WYOMING HIT

A con with a fast draw and a grudge was heading for town. It had only been days since his release and the bodies were already stacking up. Threats were being made and an ageing bounty hunter was brought out of retirement – the only man reckoned to be able to match the desperado's speed. Meanwhile, somebody was employing hit men, but for what reason? And who was doing the fixing? Ham Johnson couldn't figure it out. He had served his time and his only aim was to get out of Wyoming Territory and start a new life...

WYOMING HIT

WYOMING HIT

by

Charles Langley Hayes

Dales Large Print Books
Long Preston, North Yorkshire,
BD23 4ND, England.

British Library Cataloguing in Publication Data.

Hayes, Charles Langley
Wyoming hit.

A catalogue record of this book is
available from the British Library

ISBN 1-84262-465-2 pbk
ISBN 978-1-84262-465-4 pbk

First published in Great Britain 2005 by Robert Hale Limited

Published in Large Print 2006 by arrangement with
Robert Hale Ltd.

Dales Large Print is an imprint of Library Magna Books Ltd.

Printed and bound in Great Britain by
T.J. (International) Ltd., Cornwall, PL28 8RW

For Chris

ONE

Later on he worked out why he had been jumped, but at the time Ham Johnson hadn't got a clue.

The noon sun was striking him and his horse when he reined in atop a ridge and took off his Stetson. As he took in the scene he knuckled some sweat from his eyebrow, the one with the white slit across it marking a knife slash laid there during his hectic early days. Huh, the guy had started the scrap with a knife but when it was over the only thing the bozo needed was a spade.

He replaced his hat when he caught the glitter of reflected light down below on the flat; the green surrounding the spot told him it was water. With his canteen empty, he nudged his horse down the slope towards the welcome sight. The pinto caught the scent, whinnied and broke into a trot.

Up close Ham could see it was a small stream: a good sign. Stagnant water was always chancy but running water was a good bet. Passing a clump of mesquite, he fell out of the saddle and bellied down alongside the horse that had already lowered its head and was lapping voraciously.

Ham tasted a sample, seemed OK, then took refreshing gulps. When he'd had his fill he took off his neckerchief, soaked it and wiped it over his face.

He untied his canteen and had just lowered it into the stream when a rifle shattered the silence and his horse keeled over, crashing into the water. Dropping his canteen, Ham crouched low and drew his gun, his eyes raking the environs.

But he could see no one. He was out in the open far from cover, so the bushwhacker was somewhere in the distant rocks and, from that distance, had to be using a rifle.

Another round spanged into the soil beside him and he sought cover behind the bulk of his now dead horse. Yet another slug zipped into the water beside him. Where the hell was the bastard?

Wherever the critter was, it was clear the horse offered little protection against the onslaught of lead. He looked around, yanking at the reins of his racing mind in an attempt to glean some clue of the slugs' source from their trajectory. Yes, thinking of them in combination he was pretty sure they could only have come from the western side of the flats. He looked towards the west, then caught the reflection of sun on metal as another round was sent his way. He glanced about. The only protection from that direction was the mesquite but it was some yards back.

Nothing for it. He hauled his rifle out of the saddle boot and made a dash for the shrub. He had almost made it when something scorched his arm. He gave an exaggerated scream and flipped over to land partly under cover – but at least he was on the protective side of the vegetation.

In the circumstances the only ploy was to play possum. So, making sure that the visible part of his body remained motionless, he jacked a load into his rifle, lined it up and waited.

For a long time he sensed nothing but his own heartbeat and the buzzing of insects. Then, a distant voice: 'Is he dead?'

'Looks like it.'

So there was more than one bushwhacking bastard. But how many in total? At least the clarity of their voices indicated they had broken cover.

'Go and check, Sunny. I'll cover you.'

From the wording of the instruction Ham sensed that the number was no more than two. After a time, he heard the splash of water as someone crossed the shallow stream. Then nearer, the slow crunch of boots on gravel. Ham's fingers crawled across the sand, this way and that, until they gripped a small rock. Then he bided his time. Eventually the sounds of movement became slower and more considered indicating that the man approaching was taking even more care; and so the varmint had to be real close.

Ham held his breath, leaving any action as long as he dared, then hurled the rock to the right and promptly rolled to the left. Not knowing at first precisely where the man would be, he just triggered repeatedly in the estimated direction. At least one shell had caught the fellow because by the time Ham had a clear view of his target, the man was careering backwards.

The fellow's gun sent a round into the air, as Ham put another slug into his body. With the other of his attackers still not located, Ham rolled back into cover and jacked in new loads. Peering around the mesquite he could see a man out in the open, running hell for leather back to the rocks. Ham loped forwards to check the fallen man; the hole in the forehead was enough to tell him that one was no longer a threat. Then he dropped to one knee, took careful aim at the receding figure. With the slow confidence of a man who knew what he was doing, he lined up and triggered. The distant man sprawled forward.

Keeping his rifle levelled, Ham splashed across the stream and approached. The man was groaning.

Ham wrenched the rifle from the man's grip and flung it some yards away.

'Why the hell was you trying to put out my lights?' he snarled, as he heaved the man onto his back and removed the fellow's pistol from its holster.

The man grunted with pain, then spoke slowly. 'Nothing personal, mister. Just a way of roping in a few dollars.'

'Roping in a few dollars? Hell of a way to earn a living, *amigo*. Well, if you pulled this stunt to rob me, you picked the wrong man. First, I don't take kindly to being jumped and as you can see to your cost, I can handle myself. Second, all I got is an empty wallet. Fact, ain't got nothing but that hoss you shot. And, you shithead, I ain't even got that now 'cos of you.'

The man slowly shook his head. 'No, we wasn't aiming to fleece you: we got paid to *stop* you.'

'There's stopping and stopping.'

'We was paid to stop you – permanent.'

'Permanent? That's a mite extreme. Who by?'

The man didn't answer.

'Listen, bub,' Ham said, 'the state you're in, ain't much to be gained by keeping quiet.'

The man thought about it and muttered, 'Josh Arnold.'

'Never heard of him. Who's he?'

'Some guy over in Julesburg.'

'So why did he want me out of the way?'

'Didn't say.'

'Ain't there nothing you can tell me about this caper?'

'I've told you all I know.' He coughed, and blood frothed at his mouth. 'How's Sunny Joe?'

'Sunny Joe? He your pardner down there?'

'Yeah. Sunny Joe Williams.'

'Well, he ain't so sunny no more.'

'You mean he's bought it?'

'He didn't exactly buy it. I *gave* it to him. Free of charge. But, however you want to put it, he's a man with no future. Now we're getting all sociable and making introductions, who are you?'

'Bill Hodder.' He coughed again, wiped his hand across his lips and examined the redness with wavering eyes. 'Listen, mister, you gotta get me to a doctor.'

Ham laughed. 'With regard to your current predicament, you're on your own, Bill. Like you said earlier, nothing personal.'

He looked up at the rocks. 'I'm shy of a horse. I figure your mounts are up there. Right?'

The man nodded and closed his eyes.

It took some time for Ham to locate the two horses and by the time he was back on the flats, the man called Hodder had coughed his last.

At the stream Ham eased off his jacket and examined his own injury. More of a bullet burn than an open wound. He hunkered down, built a smoke and reflected on the events. He could think of no reason why anybody – this Josh Arnold or anybody else – should want him dead. The business didn't make sense. In fact, he was hard pressed to think of anybody who would hold a grudge against him. Not a bullet in the gut and 'nail him down in a wooden box' type of grudge. He'd done nobody down. Not in living memory. It wasn't his style. OK, he was a lawbreaker, but he was a straight one. He'd just done three years and hadn't spilled the beans on his pardners. They would know that, because if he had struck a deal and gone State's Evidence, the law would have been after *them* and he wouldn't have had to spend that length of time in stir. So his erstwhile *compadres* had every reason to be *grateful*. Nothing made sense.

And who was this Josh Arnold? He stubbed out his smoke and considered the two corpses littering the landscape. Their deaths didn't bother him. They deserved it.

Ending a life was no new experience for him. He usually managed it face to face. That way if the law finally collared him, he could get away with self-defence. At worst manslaughter, and he'd done time for that. But he'd paid all his dues. With that background, two new corpses weren't on his conscience.

His first impulse was to play it above board, take them in to the nearest town and explain how he had been bushwhacked. A first step in becoming a regular citizen. But the more he thought about it, the more reservations he had.

First off, he would have to give his name. He'd had his mug on reward posters in the past so there was some chance he would be recognized when calling in at a law office. In that case, suspicions would be aroused about the killings if he threw in a false name when reporting them. That was a spot he did not hanker to get embroiled in.

Moreover, he remembered the warden's last words back in Laramie Pen. The slightest trouble over the next year and he would be back inside. And two dead men with his bullets in them constituted a shade more than 'slight trouble'.

Then, what about this Josh Arnold? The guy had some unknown but strong reason for wanting Ham out of the way. If the guy had had the money to pay killers, he would surely have the money to finance further attempts once he learned that the first try had been unsuccessful. Whatever his reason.

Yes, finally, we come to the reason. Ham couldn't rest easy until he knew the reason why he had been at the wrong end of a couple of gun barrels. Indeed, he'd be itchy until, one way or another, he had sorted out this Arnold guy, whoever he was.

Where could he locate the schmuck? The man had said Julesburg. But just because that's where the contract had been arranged didn't mean the guy could still be found there. Ham knew the place but hadn't heard of a Josh Arnold there. He thought on it. The place wasn't far out of his way. Would only be a slight detour. OK, Julesburg would be his new destination.

He flicked the stub of his cigarette into the stream and looked at his hands; hands that had done nothing for three years but make brooms and furniture in the prison workshop. However the recent escapade had taught him one thing: it let him know that they had still retained the skills to operate weaponry when the need arose.

Three years. Three long years, that would have been even longer had not Laramie Penitentiary been overcrowded. The place was developing a name for its cramped conditions and consequent disease, a worry to the authorities who were anticipating statehood in the not too distant future. So, a commission has been set up to investigate the problem. Their answer was a new, larger prison out at Rawlins. That should meet the Federal Government's requirements and show that Wyoming was capable of handling its own affairs. But the building of the new facility would take years and the commission was given power to take whatever steps they thought necessary in the interim. So, to this end, they had begun a programme of shipping prisoners out of the territory to other territorial and state prisons. However, not only was this expensive but, with the increase in crime, even this measure was not enough to make the conditions in Laramie respectable so the warden was given special power to arrange some early paroles at his discretion.

Although a die-hard criminal with a temper, Johnson had done time before and knew the game. It had been difficult, but he managed to keep his nose clean while inside. In fact he only lost his temper once. A fellow-con had wielded a knife during an argument. Ham had wrenched the thing from his hand and stuck it in the guy's belly. There was such a rush of blood it was plain the guy was not going to last. It was the bozo's own fault; he had crossed Ham one time too many and had it coming. Only snag was, the thing had been witnessed by another inmate. Quick thinking, Ham had drawn his own hidden knife, slit the guy's throat, shoved the blades into the hands of the two dead men and left the scene screaming that there was a fight going on and for someone to intervene. Nobody questioned what their eyes told them.

And so it was that during his stretch, Ham came up with a clean slate; the result being he had been selected as one of the warden's special parolees.

Which gave him an extra reason not to want a couple of new stiffs on his record. He stood up and glanced around the ragged terrain. Shouldn't be too much of problem to dispose of them.

He found a deep gap between obelisks up in the rocks that provided a natural grave into which he dumped the mortal remains of the two bushwhackers. Without the proper tools it took him some time to cover them with soil and gravel, but eventually the task was complete to his satisfaction.

He looked down as he scooped the last

earth onto the mound and shook his head. Incompetent pissants. They didn't know what they were letting themselves in for, trying to drygulch one of the best men with a gun this side of the Missouri.

He heavy-footed back to the flat, appraised the bushwhackers' animals, choosing a white-flecked grey as his saddle horse, and mounted up.

Look on the bright side, he said to himself as he headed out. Apart from the puzzle that had been thrown up, it hadn't proved too bad a day. For starters, he now had an extra horse. That would fetch a few bucks at the first opportunity. Plus he had stripped the bodies of all valuables and money, the latter amounting to several hundred dollars, presumably the contract money. As he'd been sent out from prison into the wide world with only the stipulated twenty dollars provided by the Territory, that was a real bonus.

A Union Pacific Railroad surveyor had been

adjusting his theodolite when he had heard gunfire. It was muffled and distant so that for a time he couldn't locate the source. He clambered to the top of the nearest ridge. Eventually he could make out movement but he was too far away to discern details. He returned to his pack horse and took his telescope out of a saddle-bag. By the time he had remounted the ridge he couldn't see any movement but his glass did enable him to identify the body of a horse partway into a stream.

He swung the lens around the terrain this way and that until he spotted some movement in the rocks. A man was dragging a still figure up the slope!

With an extra layer of sweat dripping from his brow the surveyor hunkered down a little to minimize the chance of being spotted himself. There had been some shooting out there and a man was burying two bodies in the rocks; the railroad man didn't want to make himself the third body.

He kept out of sight, only chancing a

cautious peer over the edge from time to time to monitor developments. His main priority now was to learn in which direction the killer would be headed, so they didn't cross trails.

He watched the man finish his grisly task, descend and ride out with two horses – towards him!

His heart thumping, he kept the lens on the approaching figure as long as he dared. Couldn't make out much of the man's features, but he was riding a grey and it seemed like the animal had different colouring across its forehead. A white flash, he reckoned.

But he didn't wait to make any more observations and scrambled down the slope. He untethered his own horses and led them, angling round the rock formation away from the side where the gunman would be passing. Getting his animals out of sight in a thicket he waited. Eventually he saw the man riding slowly by. Thankfully the man turned away, heading north, opposite to the trail on which surveyor hoped to go.

He waited until the man had completely disappeared and manoeuvred his horses down the grade. Mounting up he headed back to his base at Tie Siding.

It was late afternoon dark when the surveyor rode along the side of the log-filled river that led to Tie Siding. The drone of buzzsaws greeted his ears as he entered the mud track between the shacks that constituted the main drag. With its main function being the production of ties for Union Pacific, the place was more of a company settlement than a town. As a result it didn't have a law office but the railroad police had an agent there. As a fellow company man, the surveyor knew him well and headed straight for the man's office to relay his findings.

'Ain't on railroad property so ain't any of my business,' the railroad policeman said when the story had been recounted. 'But, as you know, we liaise closely with civil law so just show me where you saw this shooting so that I can telegraph the Albany County law office.'

The surveyor disappeared outside and returned with a map which he unrolled on the desk. He pointed to a spot. 'Exactly there. Near a stream.' He took out a pencil and marked a cross. 'And the bodies were hidden in a fissure of striated carboniferous rock, right there.'

The railroad lawman chuckled. 'I can sure see I'm asking the right fellow.'

'Tell 'em they can't miss the location,' the surveyor added. 'There's the cadaver of a horse in the stream.'

TWO

The six riders drew rein as the dog came from the small complex of buildings, snapping its challenges at them. Although a gutsy little tyke, the animal knew its limits when faced with such a large group and kept its distance, satisfying itself with a continuous growl.

One of the men drew his gun and blasted. The dog yelped and crumpled, its bark transmuting into a whimper.

'Let's hope nobody heard that,' one of the other riders said, glancing about as the sound ricocheted around the flat landscape.

'Hell, what did you have to do that for anyways?' another said. 'We could have roped the mutt and tied it up someplace.'

The young lad with the gun sheathed his weapon, took off his hat and ran a hand over his close-cropped head. As he did so his shirtsleeve fell back a little, partly exposing the tattoo of a Confederate flag. 'Jeez, what's wrong with you guys? Problem's solved, ain't it?'

One of the others grunted. 'Seems to me you ain't gonna be happy till you've shot or maimed every critter on God's earth that moves or wriggles.' He dismounted and studied the dog, now unable to stand with its half shot-away leg, eyes closed, a staccato of pathetic snuffles emanating from its clamped jaws.

'See, you ain't even killed it,' he grunted and dispatched the animal with one shot from his own gun. 'Now let's get busy.'

Mo Fuller manoeuvred the four-horse wagon down the grade and onto the flats.

He was not the most intelligent of men. Half-witted – that was the technical term a doctor had used to describe him, and what folks had called him ever since. But he had enough brain cells to handle his job. His sole responsibility was to ensure that the water tower at the railroad halt was full. This he did by collecting water from a pool in the hills and bringing it down in the wagon.

For his work he received free accommodation and food, which naturally came by train, along with twenty dollars a month. Stuck out in the middle of nowhere, he had no immediate need of the money, which was paid to his mother in Denver who banked it for him.

He pulled in at the halt. His world was confined to the water tower and a shack for stabling the horses with his bed in a lean-to against the stable. It was a little world but it satisfied him. Meant he didn't have to mix with folk. He just didn't cotton to folk – ever since his schooldays they had always ridiculed him because of his slowness – and now, in his adult years, he had become accustomed to achieving a certain degree of happiness with his own company. And that of his dog.

His pet could hear the crunch of wagon

wheels half a mile away and would come to greet him, yet today there was no sign.

On his return to the place that he called home his first task was to unharness the horses, water and feed them with the grain supplied by the railroad.

That was his ritual but today his first concern was the whereabouts of his dog.

He pulled in and dropped down from the seat. Strange; he thought he caught the faint snicker of a horse coming from the stable. No, that couldn't be so. Must have been some odd sound coming in on the wind from the flats. Living alone in the wilderness, sometimes your ears could play tricks.

He dismissed it and called out for his dog. That his pet hadn't come a-yapping in greeting was strange. Real strange. But even stranger was the gun muzzle that suddenly pointed at him as he rounded one of the buildings.

Something hit him from behind and when he came to he was bound and gagged in the stable. He groaned as his senses returned, his first thought being 'Hell, I just don't like people.'

As his brain started to get a grip, he remembered his missing dog. Concern for the animal mounted when he heard a whistle-blast; then the sound of brakeshoes whining and the mighty bell-stacker jerking to a halt.

And now something else was happening outside. He could hear low voices and fast-moving feet.

Outside, the six masked men broke cover each setting about his allotted task. One covered the engineer and his assistant as they debouched from the now stationary train. One mounted the ladder of the passenger car. Two covered the sides of the train from the ground. One entered the passenger car, another the caboose.

The one on the roof smashed the glass of a skylight. 'Stay calm,' he shouted down into the car. 'Nobody move and nobody gets hurt.' Then he lit a stick of dynamite and hurled it at the base of the water tower. The explosion brought the thing crashing down, simultaneously blowing in carriage windows. Horses whinnied and passengers screamed at the explosion.

'There's a man on the roof of the passenger car with another stick,' the one in the caboose yelled at the officials. 'Any trouble and he drops that one in. Then you'll have a carfull of dead passengers on your hands. Now open that safe.'

Meanwhile the same threat was presented to the passengers who quickly complied by handing over their money and valuables to the masked man walking down the aisle.

The explosion had done its job. Both passengers and railroad personnel were terrified. No one raised any opposition.

The result: minutes later the six masked men were clear and heading for the hills.

THREE

Archie Royal stepped onto the boardwalk and pressed fingers against the nervous pulse that had begun its drum-roll in his temple ever since he had heard the news.

He knocked the door of the Julesburg law office and entered.

Sheriff Connor was working at his desk. 'Archie, good to see you,' he said, looking up. 'What can I do for you?'

'A lot I hope.'

The sheriff gestured to his deputy. 'Dink, get a chair for Mr Royal.' Then to the visitor: 'Sit down, Archie. Tell me what.'

Royal dropped into the chair that the young deputy provided. He took off his hat and wiped his brow. 'He's out, Lee.'

'Who's out?'

'Ham Johnson.'

Sheriff Lee Connor picked up his chunky cherry-wood pipe and poked at the dottle. 'I didn't know.' He thought some. 'Don't seem like four years.'

'It ain't. It's three. Been let out under some new scheme.'

'OK, he's out – so what?'

'I was a witness who put him away.'

The other laughed. 'Don't worry, Archie. For Christ's sake, half the town saw him and testified in court. You were only one among many. He has no need to single you out.'

'Yeah, but have they had threats?'

'Not that I know of.'

'There you are. I have.'

The sheriff lit his pipe, his cheeks becoming hollow as he drew hard. 'I didn't know. You didn't tell me.'

'I only had the threat two days ago. Then this morning, I got word he was out. Things are happening fast.'

The lawman took the pipe from his mouth and examined the glowing embers while he considered the matter. 'Tell me more about this threat you've had.'

'One of his cellmates got out a few days before Johnson. He was riding this way and stopped by at my place to warn me what he'd heard. Said how Johnson had kept on about how he couldn't wait to get out and pay me back.'

Puzzle lines marked the sheriff's forehead. 'Johnson had named you specifically? There's no mix-up?'

'"Archie Royal", this ex-con had said. How many Archie Royals are there in Wyoming? It's me all right. Besides, it was Johnson's making it clear who I was and where I lived is how this fellow convict knew exactly where to find me.'

The sheriff watched smoke rise to the ceiling, then asked, 'This guy who came a-calling, you pay him anything?'

'Gave him fifty dollars for his trouble. Figured it was mighty friendly of him to go out of his way to tell me.'

The sheriff nodded. 'There you are. This fellow coming out of stir and shy of a dollar, he just saw you as an easy touch. Over three years Johnson probably mentioned you – simply in passing – and this con made up the tale, seeing an opportunity to make a quick buck.' He grunted. 'Or more specifically, a quick fifty.'

Royal started nibbling determinedly at his nails. 'There's got to be more to it than that, Lee.'

'Listen, Archie, it is my opinion that you're getting yourself all fretted up over nothing. This con squeezed you for some dough. That's all. Even if there was something in it, you got a passel of ranch hands out at that spread of yours.'

'Yeah. And they're exactly that: ranch hands. They're not capable of standing up to a hardcase gunny like Johnson on the prod. You know what he's like with a gun.'

'OK, Archie,' the sheriff said. He gestured towards his deputy. 'Dink here and me'll keep a look-out for Johnson. If we see him, we'll speak to him, let him know that we know he's in town and we've heard of the threat.'

'That all you can offer?'

The sheriff shrugged. 'If he's out, he's paid his debt to society and he's as free as you or me. I can't touch him till he's actually done something. That's the way the law works.'

'Then it might be too late.'

'Hell, Archie, what else do you expect me to do?'

'Give me some protection.'

The sheriff chuckled humourlessly. 'Archie, you know there's only me and Dink here. There's a premium on our time as it is. I'm afraid, much as I would like to help out a taxpayer and a pal, we can't spare time taking it in turns to be your personal bodyguard.'

'That all you got to say?'

'Sorry, Arch, but there's nothing else I can do. I just ain't got the resources. It's blood out of a stone trying to get funds out of the town council.'

Rejoining his men who had been waiting for him on the boardwalk outside, Royal looked up and down the street, then caught sight of the shingle proclaiming *The Julesburg Courier*. 'Come on, boys. I got an idea.'

Seconds later he was in the printer's office. 'How long would it take you to print a couple of dozen posters?' he asked the man with the green eyeshade.

The printer threw a glance at his visitor then looked at his schedule on the notice-board. 'Afraid we're real busy at the moment, Mr Royal,' he shouted above the sound of the letterpress machine clanking in the back. 'It'd be a couple of days.'

The ranch owner took out his bill-fold. 'You produce them in half an hour and you can name your price.'

The newspaperman pushed his eyeshade up a few inches. 'OK, if you're willing to pay me top-dollar compensation I'll drop everything. But we're talking about an hour. Now, how big do you want this poster and what's the copy?'

'Copy?'

'That means what do you want it to say?'

Later in the day, Dink Talbot rushed into

the law office. 'I think you might be interested, boss. Mr Royal and his boys are slapping up posters all over town.'

'What's it about?'

'Come and see for yourself. They've put one on our board.'

Outside the sheriff ran his eye over the poster.

$500 for the Apprehension of
Ham Johnson.
Authorized by A. Royal, Crown Ranch.

He tore it down and went in search of the ranch-owner. He found him at the end of town where one of his crew was tacking another copy to a telegraph pole.

'Hold your horses, Archie. You can't do that.'

'Why not? You tell me the law can't help.'

'Johnson is a free man and not wanted for an offence.'

'Hell, Lee. He's threatened me.'

'It's an *alleged* threat, hearsay to boot. And

you can't put a price on his hide.'

'It's not a price on his hide; it's an offer of payment for apprehending him, not to kill him.'

'That's not the way some hardcases would see it. You persist with this and I'll have to take you in on a charge of incitement to a breaking of the peace.' He noticed a crowd gathering around them. 'Come over to the office. Meantimes, tell your men to take the posters down.'

Back in the law office, the two men sat facing each other. 'I can see you ain't gonna be settled until you feel you've got some security,' the sheriff said. 'I got an idea. You could hire yourself a bodyguard. That's not contravening any law.'

The ranch owner's eyebrows rose. 'Bodyguard! That's it, a bodyguard. I can pay. You know I can.' But he became tense again and started picking at another nail. 'Trouble is, it'd take time getting hold of somebody; and then days for them to ride out here. Johnson will be way ahead of 'em.'

The sheriff relit his pipe while he pondered on the matter. 'If you want a hired gun quick, there's always old JJ.'

'JJ?'

'Yeah. JJ Washington. You probably haven't run into him. Before your time. Runs a store out at Dry Creek nowadays. Was sheriff out at there before they pensioned him off. Figured working behind a counter was a pleasurable way to spend his slowdown days. Don't know how he's doing. Maybe he would be grateful for the money.'

'An old man?'

'Yeah, but if he's retained only half the gun skills he had as a young un, he's still the fastest draw in the territory. The likes of Ham Johnson won't faze him.'

'I don't know, Lee. Can't see me resting easy relying on a grey-haired old pensioner to watch my health.'

The sheriff smiled. 'I can tell you don't know our Mr Washington. Believe me, Archie, you could do a sight worse than having him covering your back. Ain't nothing he don't know about firearms and the handling of them. Ex-soldier and, in his time, done spells as shotgun rider, bank guard. Bounty hunter, too, before he became a lawman. He's a quiet man and not one to brag, but if he'd carved a notch on his gun handle for every hardcase he planted, it'd be down to the metal frame.'

The ranchman grunted dismissively. 'All those jobs? Sounds like a jack of all trades and master of none.'

'Funny you should use that word – master. He'd got such a rep in his day as a hunter that folks in the business called him The Gunmaster.'

He noted the look of apprehension still contorting his visitor's face. 'Listen, Archie, if it'll make you feel better, I'll tell you how to get out to his place and you can make your own decision about him. But I tell you, his missus has corralled him into a purely domestic life, so your new problem might be having to persuade *him* to take on the job. Mention my name. Tell him it's on my recommendation. Might help.'

The ranchman took a watch from his vest pocket and checked it against the banjo-clock on the wall. 'Dry Creek. There's still time to get out there today.' He stood up. 'I'll take your advice. And thanks, Lee.'

'My pleasure, Archie. And don't worry so much. I'm sure there's nothing in it.'

'What's this Johnson business all about, Lee?' the deputy asked, when the door had finally closed behind their visitor.

'It was before you pinned that badge to your vest. You remember a few years back, three desperadoes knocked off the bank here in town?'

'Yeah.'

'Well, something went wrong at the last minute and there was shooting. Nobody got hurt, save one of the gang who took a bullet, but because of the ruckus, by the time they had mounted up and were heading out, half the town saw them. Ham Johnson had already got his face on some old dodgers and he was the only one who was recognized.

Pulling a posse together took me more time than I expected; everybody wants law and order but when it comes to the crunch nobody has the time. So in the meantime I sent Wes Smith out ahead, you know the old tracker. So, by the time I'd got a bunch together and we were heading out, we'd lost the trail. Met Wes coming back. Said he's tracked them to an old disused cabin. Seems like they'd pulled in to rest and divvy up. Anyways, they spotted him and some lead was exchanged. While he was returning to inform us he looked back and saw smoke. By the time we got there, the place was ablaze. I figure in the panic of the shooting, there must have been some accident with a stove, or maybe some argument over the divvy. Who knows? Anyway they'd got the hell out. In the morning I examined what was left of the place. The cabin was a charred shell. The one who had been wounded was lying nearby, dead from his wound. Nobody could tie a name to him. Apart from that, found nothing save the remains of burnt bills blowing in the wind.'

'So they got away with nothing?'

'Yeah,' the sheriff said, standing up and moving over to a cabinet. He leafed through some documents, eventually extracting one.

'When we got back to town,' he went on, 'I got these wanted posters out and showed them around including that one.' He handed the fading document to his deputy.

Dink nodded as he perused it. 'Ham Johnson. Wanted for murder in El Paso.'

'Yeah. He'd got caught on that job, charge reduced to manslaughter as I recall and he'd served a short sentence. Long time since. But I never throw those things away, even when a varmint's been caught. Never know when they might come in useful. Like that one. Anyways, as a result Johnson was picked up out in Arizona shortly afterwards. Broke and hoboing around. He was brought back and stood trial here under the circuit judge. He had no defence as a passel of townsfolk identified him. One of the old school, he refused to name his confederates and got the full four years.'

'And Archie Royal was one.'

'Yeah. Archie had just done some business in the bank and so was one of those up close when the gang came storming out. But as you heard, I reminded Archie there was at least half a dozen who testified. I can't see any reason why Johnson would single out just him for revenge.'

Dink studied the poster some more then dropped it on the desk. He walked slowly to the end of the office, then whirled round drawing his gun. He made pretence of firing it a couple of times, then blew imaginary smoke from the barrel. Finally, he spun the weapon adroitly on its trigger guard and snapped it back into its holster.

The sheriff rolled his eyes disdainfully at the display.

The younger man nodded at the poster on the desk. 'I'd be a match for that Johnson any day. Can't see why you didn't give me the job of body-guarding Mr Royal for a spell. I could handle it.'

'Oh, yeah – then I could chisel on your gravestone: "I thought I could handle it". Your ma would thank me for that.' He puffed on his pipe. 'Besides, I've told you before, we have a duty to all citizens. It's not our job to offer personal full-time protection to one.'

Dink picked up the poster again. 'This guy coming to town could liven things up a piece, boss. Make a change from doing nothing more exciting than locking up drunks on a Saturday night.'

The sheriff shook his head. 'I've knowed your ma since we was learning our letters in the schoolhouse together. Then, after your pa died, I've watched her trying to cope with you. The town's little big-shot. All kids are trouble but you took the biscuit with your bragging, scrapping and just being ornery for the sake of it. Then the prancing round town, flashing your gun. And the scrapes I've had to get you out of for your ma's sake. That's why I offered to take you under my wing. Provide you with a regular job so you'd learn some discipline, keep out of trouble and have some dollars to take home to your ma. And so far, Dink, you've toed the line. Been a credit to your ma and to my judgement. Don't spoil it by getting some danged fool idea in your head. If you spot this Johnson in town, you don't do nothing; you just tell me.'

'Anything you say, boss.'

FOUR

Mrs Emma Washington was sweeping the floor when the bell on the spring above the door rang.

'Good day, Mrs Jones,' she said when she recognized her visitor. 'And what can I do for you?'

'I want to make a couple of dresses,' the customer explained. 'What material do you have?'

Mrs Washington pointed to the rolls on the shelves behind her. 'Choice of three. Calico, homespun. Then there's the linen damask if you want some colour. See, an attractive red.'

The prospective customer considered the fabrics. 'Is that all? Pity. I am in need of something singular. We're going to a wedding and I wanted to run up something special. I rather fancy blue.'

'No problem,' the proprietress said. 'There's quite a range in the catalogue. You pick what you need and your order will be winging its way out of town on the afternoon coach.'

'No. That will take too long. I was hoping to start on it today. Makes no never-mind. I've still got a wardrobe of dresses. I'll make something up from one of them.' Then, with a 'Good day', she was gone.

At that point Mrs Washington's husband came in from the back with some bags of coffee beans.

'Heard the bell go,' he said. 'Another

satisfied customer?'

'Another *dis*satisfied customer,' his wife retorted. 'Wanted some fabric but couldn't wait for us to order through the catalogue. I've told you before, JJ, we lose a lot of business by not having much by way of stocks. The more you got on display the more folk are likely to see something to buy. Sending away to Denver for stuff makes a big deal out of it and allows them to have second thoughts. Then you lose the sale.'

He placed the bean bags neatly on a shelf. 'I know, Em, but stocks cost money. We make enough to get by, but not enough to buy in much by way of extra stocks. You know business ain't been too good lately. Besides we need to get someone to repaint the sign outside. I've noticed it's looking mighty weather-beaten these days.'

She chuckled. 'You only want it repainted because we never got around to putting your name on it.'

'Shucks, Em. I ain't bothered about seeing my name out there. But the fact is, peeling away the way it is, ain't likely to attract trade.'

'Like you said, that'll cost money.'

He patted dust from his hands and put them to his nose. 'Hmm, smelling those beans puts me in mind of a cup of coffee.'

'You watch the shop a while,' his wife said. 'I'll make some fresh.'

Alone in the store, he pottered around until the bell rang again. The door opened to reveal a large man blocking the frame.

'JJ! How you doing?'

'Well, I'll be. If it ain't Big John McBride.'

The big man strode across the floor and shook the older man's hand vigorously. 'Good to see you, JJ.'

'What can I do for you?'

The visitor indicated a roll of papers in his hand. 'My manager and me, we're putting these posters around town. Would you put one up in here?'

Johnny McBride was an old friend, a blacksmith over in Julesburg. However from time to time he would take time off to prizefight, using the sobriquet of Hard Rock McBride. However to his friends he remained Johnny or Big John.

The older man walked across to a board already dotted with assorted notices. 'Of course. I'll make space.' He scanned the existing posters and took the opportunity to remove out-dated ones.

'Can you make the fight?' Big John asked, after he had fixed the billing. 'There's a free ticket waiting for you. I can do with all the support I can get.'

The oldster read the specifics. It detailed a fight two days hence in Julesburg.

The old-timer tapped the name of his opponent. 'Who's this Killer Garfield?'

'Some big-mouth.'

'Says he's the Champion of the Mid-West.'

'Don't believe everything you read, JJ.'

'Killer, too.'

'They gotta call him something flashy to get the punters in. You know that. It's all flim-flam.'

'You mean like Hard Rock?'

The other chuckled. 'Yeah.'

'Seriously, Johnny. Can you handle him?'

'With one arm tied behind my back. Especially with a home crowd behind me. I've told you: he's a nobody. Can't imagine anybody even betting on him.'

At this point the lady came in with coffee.

'Hi, there, Mrs Washington.'

'Hello, Johnny. Nice to see you. Can you handle some coffee, young man?'

'No, thank you kindly, Mrs Washington,' the visitor said, heading for the door. 'I got the rest of these posters to fix.'

'Good to see you, Johnny,' JJ said. 'Can't see me being able to make the fight, but all the best on the night.'

He was just about to lock up for the day when a final caller pushed through the door.

'Mr JJ Washington?' the man asked.

JJ looked him over. The man had a small pinched-up mouth and eyes that glared from under shaggy eyebrows. Not an attractive prospect, but the suit and its cut said the fellow had money.

'Yes, sir. What can I do for you?'

'Name's Archie Royal. Own the Royal Crown Ranch the other side of Julesburg.'

JJ nodded. 'I heard of the outfit.'

'I've come over on the recommendation of Lee Connor, the sheriff over there.'

'I know Lee, yeah. How is he?'

'He's fine. Sends his regards. The point is, he tells me you've had some experience with a gun.'

JJ shrugged non-commitally. 'I know which end the bullet comes out.'

Royal went on to explain his problem. 'So,' he concluded, 'I'm here making a request for your services.'

JJ waved his hands round the store. 'I'm afraid you've had a wasted journey. Mr Royal. This is my life now. Lee Connor knows that. Can't think why he would recommend me.'

'Because I'm stuck and he says you're the only one in the territory who could handle

Ham Johnson. He's something of a hardcase – and real mean with a gun.'

JJ went to a shelf lined with jars of varied tobacco products and took a cigar from one. He offered one to his visitor who politely declined. The storekeeper remained silent while he rolled the cigar between his lips, then lit it. He shook his head. 'Those days are over.'

'I'll pay you for your time. I'm sure we can hit on a mutually acceptable fee. I'm not a poor man.'

JJ exhaled some more smoke. 'You come a long ways. Least I can do is think about it some.' He looked at the ash on the end of the cigar while he contemplated, then said, 'Tell you what: let me have few words in private in back with my missus.'

'Em,' he said, when he got to the kitchen where his wife was preparing vegetables for the evening meal. 'These fabrics you were a-talking of. How much would you need to build up a good stock?'

'The stuff don't come cheap, JJ. I guess

we'd need a hundred to provide a basic range.'

'And how much if you went beyond basics?'

She looked puzzled. 'Well, if we got in some associated trappings, you know lace edgings and a few rolls of real luxury stuff, it would push the bill up to over two hundred.'

He puffed on his pipe. 'Say another hundred to extend our lines into some fancy goods,' he added. 'Like you say, Em, a well-stocked store is attractive and can encourage purchasing. Then, maybe, fifty to get a new sign painted and a lick of new paint over the front. I figure five hundred in total would do it, wouldn't you?'

'Five hundred? Are you out of your mind, JJ? We haven't got that kind money. And I don't cotton to going into hock with the bank.'

As he explained about the ranch-owner's offer she stopped working. 'Ever since I talked you out of your dangerous occupation,' she said when he'd finished, 'I been sensing you getting fiddle-footed. But, much as we could do with the money, I don't want you putting yourself at risk again.'

'It'll just be a one-off, Em, and on my terms.'

She wiped her hands and sat down at the kitchen table. 'I can see you've got your mind set, JJ,' she concluded after some contemplation. 'You make your own decision. If you say yes, just promise me it won't mean that you'll be taking to the bounty trail permanent again.'

He put his arm round her. 'What? And miss your cooking? Thanks for being understanding, Em.'

Back in the front he eyed his visitor. 'When I was chasing bounties, Mr Royal, I never risked life and limb for less than a thousand dollars. That's my fee. A fixed sum, whether it takes a month or a few days.'

It was a deal more than the ranch owner had anticipated and he paused for moment while the figure sank in. Then: 'OK, it's a deal, Mr Washington.'

'And two hundred up front.'

Royal nodded and put out his hand. After they had shaken, he pulled out his wallet. 'I can let you have a hundred in bills and make up the difference with a bank draft, cashable at the Dry Creek bank in the morning.'

'That's acceptable,' JJ said, as he pulled out a couple of chairs. 'Now let's talk details. Tell me as much as you know.'

'OK,' he said, when the other had finished his account of the convict and the relayed threat. 'I do the job my way. For a start, waiting for this Ham Johnson to make his play will give him the advantage in choosing time and place. That's bad strategy. First, I need to know more about him. Then I go looking for him. That way, I choose time and place.'

His visitor looked concerned again. 'But what I want from you is personal protection. What happens to me while you're away investigating?'

'Don't worry, Mr Royal. Before I do any

scouting I'll come over and have a look at your place. I'll check the situation and vet your men. We should be able to make it defendable for the time that I'll be out and about.'

After Royal and his men had left, JJ returned to the kitchen and dropped the money and bank draft on the table. 'There you are, Em. You can start ordering fabric first thing in the morning. And there's going to be another eight hundred on top of that when the job's done.'

He moved to a side door. 'Now leave me be for a spell,' he said, with a conspiratorial wink.

He went to the smallest storeroom on the premises. Besides providing a little storage space for merchandise it served as his hidey-hole and workroom. A rack on the wall held long-barrelled weapons while hand pistols rested in cupboard drawers.

Each gun told a story. The .36 Savage hand pistol from his army days; the two single-shot .41 derringers, one fitting snugly into a special harness in the small of his back, the other in a compartment in a saddle-bag so skilfully contrived that only a persevering searcher would have found it. Both had come into play at one time or another when some miscreant had temporarily got the upper hand and stripped him of his visible ordnance. The Sharps buffalo gun he had used on more than one occasion to fetch down some hard-nosed varmint at over 800 paces; the Martini-Henry, given to him as parting gift by an Indian friend, now long resident in the happy hunting grounds; the .52 breech-loading Spencer, his fall-back long arm: all had seen long service. All old friends.

But he didn't need the choice. The present task was not a long-haul manhunting mission like the old days. This required just the basics. With regard to choice, there was nothing to think about. He lifted the Winchester from the rack, hefted it and laid it on one side.

From a drawer he picked up of one his .36 Navy Colts, his former inseparable companions. Its barrel, slightly shorter than that of its cousin the Army Colt, gave an edge on speed of draw. He bounced its weight in his hand, then took out its brother, reminding himself of the feel of the well-worn walnut grips.

Old habits died hard and for a long time after his retirement he had regularly cleaned and oiled all his weapons. But the practice had lapsed in recent times.

He cleared a working space and set about dismantling the three guns. The skills were still retained in his fingers but he cursed at the evidence of some stiffness in the joints as he conducted his task.

An hour on, the undertaking of cleaning and oiling was complete. He unwrapped his holsters, specially tailored for his own particular arm-length and hand configuration. He dusted their interiors, rubbing in a little oil.

Still wearing his overall he fixed the rig

around his waist, pleased that the years hadn't added any noticeable poundage to his gut so that the thing still sat comfortably in its familiar place on his hips. He hefted the Colts, once again reminding himself of their feel in his palms, and slipped them in place. With the Winchester packed in its saddle boot and boxes of ammunition in his overall pocket, he made his way out to the garbage dump on the edge of town. There were enough rusting cans around to provide target practice for a whole regiment.

He rummaged around and found a piece of planking. Placed across a couple of cardboard boxes, it provided a shelf on which to balance an array of cans.

And shortly he was blasting away at the empty tins. He didn't miss one.

FIVE

Ham Johnson rode into Julesburg. It hadn't changed much over the three years that he had been away. He pulled into The Drovers at the edge of town.

'You got a pallet for a sore ass and aching back, ma'am?'

Old Ma Cannon, the proprietress, turned at the voice, then beamed in recognition. 'Why, Ham Johnson! You son of a gun. I guessed you wus out. How long?'

'Coupla days.'

She chuckled. 'Busy coupla days!'

'What do you mean?'

'Coupla days and you've already over-drawn your account in town.'

'You're throwing me a riddle, Ma. I still don't understand.'

'Somebody told me there was dodgers

posted on you.'

His immediate reaction was to check there was no one in the sleeping quarters who could overhear. Hell, how could anyone know what had happened out at Tie Siding? he wondered. His expression changed as he considered the bleak shape of the matter. 'This poster, Ma,' he asked, 'what did it say?'

She noticed the sudden disappearance of the smile. 'Wasn't a legal poster from what I heard and didn't specify nothing in particular. Anyways, shouldn't worry none. I figure it was some kind of mistake, 'cos within half an hour of 'em going up, sheriff gave orders for them to be tore down.'

'It's got me beat, Ma.'

'I thought so by the look on your face. Maybe a case of give a dog bad name, I reckon. Anyways, lad, good to see you. Of course I got a cot. And for you, cut rate.'

'I don't aim to stay long,' he said, as she conducted him through the shack. 'Got a little business in town and then I'll be hitting the trail.'

She indicated his bed.

'And, in the light of what you've told me about this poster, I'd be obliged if it ain't common knowledge I'm in town. Don't worry, Ma. Your keeping quiet about me ain't nothing that'll put you in bad with the law. Just want to surprise one or two friends.'

She smiled. 'Hell, I ain't bothered about the law, Ham, you know that. But if it pleases you – I ain't seen yuh, *stranger*.'

He returned the smile, adding, 'Obliged.' He slung his hat onto the pallet to mark occupation. 'You heard of a guy by the name of Josh Arnold?'

She ruminated. 'Sorry, Ham. Can't say I have. It important?'

'Nothing to fret about.'

She left him to his own devices and he sat on the bed thinking. The poster couldn't have been about the killings. For a start there was no way anyone would know. And, if the matter had been as serious as murder, the poster would have made it plain and would have stayed in place. He dismissed what appeared to be a mild conundrum and turned his mind to his next step. Locating the mysterious Josh Arnold.

In any town there was a small number of occupations the incumbents of which tended, by the very nature of their business, to know the who, what and where-at of most folks in the locality. One was saloon-swamping. The conversations to which a saloon-swamper was privy were legion. But Ham didn't want to advertise his presence in town so throwing questions around saloon bars was out. He mulled over the matter. Another source was the local blacksmith. A smith's knowledge came from another perspective. He would know every man in town and the horse he rode in on.

Having come to a decision, he brought in his gear; then washed off the trail dust and headed down the drag to the smithy.

As he entered he heard thumps and saw the huge frame of Big John head down at work. Minus head and legs, the torso of a steer hung by a chain from the rafters and the fighter was hammering into it with his colossal fists. So preoccupied was the pugilist that he was unaware of the visitor.

Ham dropped his backside onto an empty saddle frame and rolled a cigarette. A few moments after he had lit up, Big John became aware of the smell. He stopped in his onslaught and turned. 'Ham! What you doing here? I thought you were pissing in a bucket.'

'And I thought *you'd* stopped prize-fighting.'

Big John clutched the carcass to stop it swinging. 'Got talked into coming out of retirement.'

'Yeah. Saw the notices as I rode in. With a name like that, Killer Garfield sounds like he's gonna present some kind of opposition.' He looked at the carcass and chuckled. 'And he ain't gonna be strung up like that poor critter. This one's gonna fight back.'

The other picked up a towel, wiped away some sweat and put the cloth around his neck. 'What can I do for you?'

'Got some names. Sunny Joe Williams. Bill Hodder. They mean anything to you?'

The blacksmith repeated the names, shaking his head, eventually concluding, 'Can't say they do.'

'Makes no never-mind. More important, you know of a Josh Arnold?'

The big man thought some more. 'Yeah. An out-of-towner. Came in some days back. Horse threw a shoe. I fixed it.'

'He pass on through?'

'Guess he's still in town.'

'You know his where-at?'

'Can't say with any exactitude, but his horse is a dun and I saw it hitched outside the Sullivan Hotel. Could be he's staying there.'

'Thanks, Big John. And best of luck for the fight.'

As he emerged once again into the sunlight Johnson heard the boxer behind him laugh and call, 'I ain't been beat yet!'

He strode down the drag. The Sullivan was a two-storey affair with a balcony running round the top. He didn't recognize the man behind the counter. 'You got a Josh Arnold staying here?'

'Who wants to know?'

Johnson leant on the counter, his face coming up close. 'I'm gonna ask you once more – politely.'

'Yes, sir. Room Seven,' the man stammered, reacting to the menace that had suddenly entered the man's tone.

'Where's that?'

'Upstairs at back, sir.'

'It opens out onto the balcony?'

'Not a door, but its window does.'

Johnson nodded, then leant further across the counter and dragged the clerk forward by his collar. 'Now I want you to do two things. You go up and knock at Number Seven. You tell Mr Arnold that Mr Laramie wants to see him and is downstairs in the lobby waiting. Mr Laramie, an acquaintance of Bill Hodder and Sunny Joe Williams. He'll understand. You got that?'

'Yes, sir,' the man faltered. 'Mr Laramie, a friend of Bill Hodder and Sunny Joe Williams.'

'No. You ain't listening. Not a friend, an *acquaintance*. He'll understand that better.'

'Yes, sir,' the man quavered. 'And the second thing?'

'Second thing: whatever happens, you don't tell nobody I was here.' He pushed the man back and tapped the butt of his gun menacingly. 'Savvy?'

'Yes, sir, I understand.'

Johnson looked at the clock and pointed at it. 'Wait two minutes, no more no less, before you go up to tell him.'

With that he left by the front entrance. Working his way round the building, he mounted the stairs at the side and walked along the balcony to the back.

Meanwhile, downstairs the proprietor was watching the clock, sensing that its ticking was louder than he had ever heard it. At the appointed time he crossed the lobby and climbed the stairs with trepidation.

He repeated the message to the guest.

'Mr Laramie?' Arnold queried, trying to mask the apprehension in his voice. 'Can't say I heard of the name. What does this fellow look like?'

'Hard to describe, sir. Big man, square-faced. Oh, one of his eyebrows had a white nick across it. Like it was a scar from some injury.'

'Which eye?'

'Er, the left, sir.'

'Thank you. Tell the gentleman I'll be down directly.'

Arnold closed the door, heart pounding. He didn't know a Mr Laramie, but he knew the other two names. And he did know somebody with a split left eyebrow, somebody who had just been released from Laramie Penitentiary. Somebody who shouldn't have the health to come walking into a hotel lobby.

Yes, he'd been down directly all right – but

not out the front.

On the balcony outside Johnson was pinned against the wall, waiting. He had heard the knock and muffled exchange of voices. A minute or so later one of the windows creaked open and a valise and bundle were quietly dropped through. Then a figure, well-cut suit and expensive hat, came easing out.

Ham waited until the man was almost out, then he simultaneously pulled the man's gun from its holster and rammed his own gun into the fellow's back.

'Come right out,' Ham growled, 'and no funny business.'

'What's this all about, mister?' Arnold whined as he stepped onto the planking, his voice carrying the feigned innocence of all crooks when they're collared.

'It ain't "mister", as you damn well know. It's Ham Johnson. And he wants to know why you paid a couple of cupcakes to have him planted.'

'I don't know what–'

The man got no further as the butt of his own gun slammed the side of his head.

'Let's start again. Reasons!'

'I didn't want you planted, Mr Johnson. They was just supposed to scare you off, is all.'

'Scare me off? They took it a mite more serious than that. Let's get round to why.'

The man looked around. There was no escape. 'It was Red Crawford paid me.'

'Red Crawford, eh?' Ham pondered on the familiar name. 'And why did he want me dealt with?'

'Didn't say.'

'You sure you can't think of a reason? See, the thing is mighty puzzling to me 'cos Red and me go back a long ways and I sure as hell can't think of any cause he would have to want me stampeded or put out of the way.'

'Don't know any more than I've told you.'

'Yeah, and what you've told me is lies. For a start, Red knows me enough to know I ain't the kind of guy to get scared off.

Second, the only reason why you would stay around here in town after the job was if you thought I had been put out of the way permanent.'

'I told you, it wasn't meant to be that way.'

'How much did he pay you?'

'Five hundred.'

'A hundred each for the two bozos leaves you with three hundred. Give me your roll.'

The man handed the money to him. Ham didn't count it – it looked pretty solid – just slipped it into his vest pocket. 'Where's he hang out these days?'

'The Lodge.'

'The Lodge? What the hell's that?'

'Big place just outa town. Red Crawford, he's the big cheese there.'

Ham paused, nodding his head. So Red had spent his cut to step up in the world. Well, he still didn't know what was going on but at least he now had a name and a place. 'That a difficult outfit to get into?'

'Like a fort. Big guys on the doors. You know Red; likes his privacy.' Then he added in a pleading tone, 'Listen, Mr Johnson, don't say nothing to him about me blabbing. He'll kill me.'

'Don't worry, pal,' Johnson said, sheathing his gun. He figured he'd got as much out of this bozo as he was going to get. He grabbed the man's wrist and rammed it up the man's back. 'I'll save him the trouble.' With his other hand he seized the man's neck, bent him forward and ran him towards the rail. The man shot over and, before he could scream, crunched head-first into the ground below.

Not bothering to investigate the effect, Ham strolled smartly along the balcony and down the steps.

The temper he had held in check for three years was re-asserting itself.

SIX

JJ got up at the crack of dawn and had got in another hour's gun practice out at the garbage dump by the time he was greeted by the smell of Em's breakfast on his return home. So it was that, after eating and to repeated pleas of 'Look after yourself', he had headed out.

Now, riding loose and easy in the saddle, he took his time journeying to the Crown. The days were gone when his trusty steed could put fifty miles of hard country behind him between sun-up and dusk. Like its owner, the critter was on the wrong side of middle age. Moreover, now mainly whiling away its time in pasture, the horse wasn't used to prolonged exercise and needed to be broken in gently.

After an eternity of flats and sagebrush, JJ

found himself amongst grazing cattle. Then a smudge in the distance, a blur which became a man.

The rider, with levelled rifle, waited until JJ came within hailing distance. 'Hold it there, mister. State your name and business.'

'JJ Washington. Mr Royal is expecting me.'

'Advance and keep your hands on the reins. Don't make any sudden movements.'

JJ did as he was bid.

'You fit the description,' the man said as JJ neared. 'Excuse the initial lack of hospitality, Mr Washington. Just didn't want to put any words into your mouth is all.' He slipped the gun into its boot and looked over his shoulder. 'It's a couple more miles to the ranch house. All hands are under instructions to be on watch. I'll ride along with you so there'll be no further impediment.'

The Crown was a huge and rambling place, displaying all the signs of a prosperous enterprise: a large adobe ranch house surrounded by well-built barns, an assortment of outbuildings and a substantial frame bunkhouse.

JJ and his escort rode past spacious pole corrals, then hitched at the rail outside the veranda of the main building.

By the time the visitor had stepped up onto the porch, Archie Royal was in the doorway. 'Mr Washington, good to see you again. Word was passed to me you were here.'

He led the way to his study and gestured to a cowhide ottoman for his visitor to use while he dropped into the high-backed swivel chair behind his desk. He ordered refreshment and sat appraising the man who had come so expensively. He had to admit that when Sheriff Connors had suggested this man, he had had misgivings. From what he could glean from the lawman's account, the fellow was in his dotage and looking back over a life spent dallying in a variety of jobs as though he had not been capable of honing and developing one specialization. Seemingly, Royal's suspicions had been confirmed when he had ridden out to Dry Gulch and seen the man in his store: nothing more than a grizzle-stubbled oldster in a brown coverall, just about capable of stacking coffee bags on shelves.

However, the figure presently sitting opposite him and similarly appraising him, was a different being, bearing no comparison to the mouse-like store-man of a few days back. Royal eyed the fellow, now dressed in trail-weathered buckskin with a brace of guns on his hips. And the ranch-owner suddenly, inexplicably, had the feeling this man knew everything and was afraid of nothing.

'You have a comfortable ride out, Mr Washington?' he began.

The visitor nodded, waved his hand dismissively and got straight down to business. 'When I've slaked my thirst, I want to get a grip on the layout here. I'd like you to show me round the immediate environs and introduce me to your workers, especially the ones closest to you.'

'Well, we can start with my foreman, Wilson here,' the ranch boss said, swivelling and indicating the man standing by the door.

Although the man had the appearance of a rough cowman, JJ noted how he took off his glove to shake hands, an elegance of attitude that was probably explained by the clipped Eastern tones of his voice. 'Pleased to make your acquaintance, sir.'

JJ pointed to the Army Colt on the man's hip. 'Good looking gun there, Mr Wilson. You can use it?'

'Would not describe myself as a sharp-shooter, sir, but I've been known to hit things I've aimed at.'

'Good.'

Some twenty minutes later, having done the rounds, the two men were back at the house standing on the veranda.

'Seems to me you got a capable bunch here,' JJ said. 'There should be no problem during daylight hours.' He dropped into a wicker chair. 'First off, you get a sheet of paper and write down all the men's names. Then, against each one you specify the particular duty for the day.'

'Like in the army.'

'Like in the army. That way, each man is clear with regard to his responsibility and there can be no disagreement should the matter arise.'

He pointed around the scene. 'It's clear you have no shortage of manpower so, come nightfall, you station a man at each out-building. They can work shifts. With regard to the ranch house itself you detail one man at each wall, with two on the veranda. You place lanterns wherever you can hang one. You keep at least two men close by. Your most trusted man is to be at your side permanently. Then, every half hour, the other does the circuit checking that all's well with the guards. Make it clear that whoever is on watch, keeps an eye on the clock. A man doesn't return within the allocated time, that could spell trouble.'

'Is that all there is to it?'

JJ nodded. 'And, with a gun under your pillow, you'll be able to get a good night's sleep.' From the beginning of their encounter he had noted that Royal had the washed-out enervation of a worried man. 'To be frank, I really don't think you've got much to fret about, Mr Royal. The way I see it, a man lines you up in his sights and fires a round in your direction, you got every right to see yourself in jeopardy. But all you got here is some tittle-tattle about a threat. By all means take it seriously, be on your guard, but don't lose sleep over it unless this man Johnson makes a positive play.'

The ranch owner's passive features suggested he found little comfort in the words.

'Which brings me to the source of this threat,' JJ went on. 'This ex-con who told you about Johnson and his supposed plans, what did he look like?'

Royal shrugged. 'Young, rangy feller. Nothing outstanding.'

'I tell you one thing,' Wilson said, 'the bum had got the Rebel flag tattooed on his arm.'

Originally from New York and a die-hard federalist, the foreman had a bent for noticing signs like that. 'The critter deserved putting in the can for that alone,' he added.

'Like I've always said,' one of his fellow-workers commented in a strong Southern drawl, 'you can take the boy out of New York but you can't take New York out of the boy.'

'Hey, you two,' Royal put in. 'The war's over.'

'The fellow was a no good,' the Northerner continued. 'Can always tell a man by his horse. A good man has a well-kept mount. But a more sorry-looking hack I never did see a man ride. The miserable bastard had given it a lashing in its time. You could tell. It had scars all over the rump.'

'Give the guy a chance,' the Southerner countered. 'Maybe he bought it that way. Just coming out of the can, the guy wouldn't have the money for a decent hoss.'

'Part of its ear was a-missing, too,' Wilson added. 'A chestnut. Must have been a good animal one time.'

'No matter,' JJ concluded. 'The fellow's probably out of the territory by now.'

He stood up and moved towards his horse. 'Well, Mr Royal, as things seem to be in place here I'll do what I can to seek out this Johnson fellow and try to stop him before he causes any trouble. I'll drop in here from time to time to check things out and keep you informed of anything I turn up.'

In town he called at the law office but the sheriff was out.

'At the funeral parlour,' the deputy explained. 'Shouldn't be long.'

It was a fine day so JJ went outside to wait, taking residence in a wicker chair on the boardwalk. Within minutes he was rewarded by the sight of his old friend crossing the street. Like JJ he had the roughed-up features of a man who had worked his way through life.

'JJ, good to see you. Come in.' Inside the lawman ambled over to the simmering coffeepot. 'Give me a minute, JJ. I can't stand the smell of that funeral parlour. The chemicals Elmer uses – ugh! Just gotta wash the smell of it out of my throat. Had to see a body before I make a report for the coroner's court. Accident. Guy fell a couple of storeys from a hotel.'

When he had finally cleared his throat to some acceptable level of satisfaction, he asked his visitor how he could be of service.

'Stopped by to thank you for floating some work my way.'

'Think nothing of it,' the lawman said, pouring himself another mug. 'With you doing nothing more adventurous than rearranging boxes in your store, I thought you might be grateful of the opportunity to get your teeth into something like this.'

'Yeah, thanks for thinking of me, Lee. Some extra money won't come amiss.'

The sheriff reflected on his own words and added with a chuckle, 'That's assuming you still got your own teeth, of course.'

JJ eyed his friend in mock rebuke. 'If we

didn't go back so long, Mr Connor, I might feel insulted by that remark.' He smiled. 'Anyways, whether or not I still got my own choppers ain't nothing to do with you.'

'I'm not being entirely altruistic,' the sheriff said in a more serious tone. 'Throwing the work your way gets Royal off my back. The guy's a real pain.' He shook his head as he mused. 'They say it takes a worried man to sing a worried song but Archie takes the biscuit.'

'Your Mr Royal is a worrit, for sure. From what I've seen of him, he doesn't seem to have what it takes to have built up a cattle empire. You know, strong personality, confidence, the kind of stuff you expect in a big businessman.'

'He didn't build it up. Inherited it from his old man. It was his pa built up the place. The old-timer was a go-getter who had a way of getting things done. And he knew about men. That's how come he established a good team of workers. Now he's gone, it's them that make sure the place runs smoothly. And you're right about Royal's disposition. Worries and frets about the smallest thing like an old woman. It's well known around town.' He chuckled. 'Doc tells me, every time there's a new illness described in a magazine, Archie's sure he's got it.'

Suddenly the door opened. JJ could tell it was the undertaker by the way the sheriff immediately screwed up his nose in anticipation.

'What is it, Elmer?' the lawman asked.

'This Josh Arnold fellow, the deceased. There's something we didn't discuss. He'd only got a few cents in his pocket.'

'That ain't a crime.'

'No. But he had no papers either. Nothing telling how we could get in contact with next of kin. So how does the funeral get paid for?'

The sheriff went to the door and opened it wide. 'You know the form. See the mayor. He'll arrange for it to be paid for out of public funds. Now for God's sake, Elmer, powder out.'

When the mortician had gone he dropped back into his chair, flapping his hand in front of his nose.

'What was all that about?' JJ asked.

'That guy I mentioned, fell from the balcony over at the Sullivan Hotel.' He suddenly hit on the idea of using his pipe as a fumigant, lit up and started belching smoke. 'Now, what we're saying?'

'Archie Royal.'

'Oh, yeah. Well, with regard to this present matter, I told Archie I didn't think there was anything to fret about. Royal was only one of a handful of witnesses. Can't see no reason on God's earth why Johnson would single him out. But he wouldn't listen.'

'That's my way of thinking, too. I told him so. But if he's got cash to throw around I ain't one to look a gift horse in the mouth.'

'That's what I thought.'

'Of course, there'll be a cut in it for you,' JJ said with a wink.

They settled down to their coffees and

brought each other up-to-date on their lives as old friends do.

'Thanks for the coffee,' JJ said in conclusion as he rose. 'Can you recommend a place where a guy can rest his bones overnight?'

'There's a guest house a block down the street. Even got a place out back for your horse.'

JJ headed for the door. 'Thanks. You'll let me know if you learn of Johnson showing up?'

'Sure. Likewise, you keep me in the picture. But I'm sure we both figure it's nothing more than a storm in a teacup.'

SEVEN

The next morning JJ slept over much longer than was his wont. The previous day had taken a lot out of him. The woman who kept the guest house was happy to prepare him a breakfast even though it was mid-morning. It was solid fare but not as good as his Em cooked. Coffee wasn't much more than coloured water either. He thought he'd begin his day by dropping in on the sheriff again. If nothing else, Lee's coffee was better.

As he stepped down from the sidewalk to cross the road, he paused to let a hearse go by. Judging by its charity appearance, must have been the accident case he'd heard about. Upfront Elmer hadn't even bothered to dress in black, a plain box wobbled in the back, while there were no mourners or flowers.

'Had an idea, Lee,' he said once he was inside the law office. 'Might be useful to send a telegraph to Laramie Pen to see if they have any knowledge of Johnson since he left. You never know. Even if they can tell us which direction he was headed in when he left, it would be something.'

'Sure thing. I'll draft a message and send Dink over with it.'

While they were taking coffee, there was a knock and a couple of men sporting badges entered. They announced themselves as federal marshals. They were on the trail of a gang of train robbers. Knocked over a bullion car on the railroad east of Denver. They'd last been seen heading west for Wyoming. Crossing state lines meant it was a federal matter. Had the sheriff or his deputy seen a gang of strangers riding through?

The sheriff shook his head. 'Sorry, guys, no. And I'm sure my deputy would have told me if he'd seen such a party.' But his fellow law officers were welcome to a cup of coffee before they rode on.

'I should take him up on the offer,' JJ threw in. 'It's good stuff.'

It had turned noon when he came out of the law office. He glanced up at the sky. Looked like rain. He had one more item of business to complete before heading for home. He made his way over to the smithy. His blacksmith friend was a good source of information and there was a good chance that if Johnson was in town Big John would know.

But the smithy was closed. 'You've just missed him, feller,' a man outside informed him. 'He's gone over to the hotel to prepare for the fight.'

'I hadn't realized the fight was tonight.'

'You must be blind, mister,' the man chuckled. 'There's enough posters over town.'

'Yeah,' JJ chuckled, 'I should have known. I've even got one of them in my store. I plumb forgot. Remind me, which hotel?'

'The Trask.'

He gave his thanks and returned to the street. The sky had darkened further. He didn't cotton to riding through a downpour. After a moment's reflection, he decided to stay over another night. His horse would be grateful for an extended rest. He went to the lean-to in back of the guest house to check his animal was OK, then returned to his room and whiled away his time while the rain pitter-pattered at the window. He took a meal and, at the appointed time, made his way over to the venue of the fight, happy to see the rain hadn't lasted.

Bathed in light and with milling crowds at the door, the Trask Hotel was unmissable in the darkness of the street. He paid the entrance fee and stepped through to the main hall. Every bench and chair in Julesburg must have been commandeered, he figured; the place was packed.

He worked his way through the crowd to a bar and bought a drink, rolling his eyes at the exorbitant price.

Around him, cigar-chomping men in fancy vests were taking bets. The odds differed slightly between the two fighters but they all favoured the home man. He placed a small bet on Big John, then looked around.

With his ancient creaking limbs he didn't cotton to standing all night. He moved along the side aisle towards the front in search of a seat but there was none vacant.

He leant against the wall and reconciled himself to standing for the full session when a dispute broke out at a front table. At first it was merely a shouted argument over the relative merits of the main boxers but the language became vituperative and a punch was thrown. Then the dispute progressed to the issue becoming resolved with the two spectators having their own impromptu bout. Egged on by those around the two went at it. Within seconds others joined in, beer was spilled, tables went over and an army of bouncers waded in.

As the main contenders were being hauled out to settle their private scrap in the street, JJ moved down and grabbed a now vacant chair. It not only provided him with a seat but it was at the front with a clear view across the limelights.

As he settled down, tables were righted and things quieted, save for the babble of anticipation amongst the audience.

A ring had been set up on the stage and eventually a couple of well-dressed gents came from the wings. The footlamps at the edge of the stage gave them a ghoulish appearance, throwing shadows from bushy eyebrows up over their foreheads. The first man raised his hands to placate the audience and announced himself as Ben Trask, proprietor of the hotel, saying how proud he was to provide the venue for the proceedings.

JJ noted the fellow's charitable demeanour, his proclamations of pride and honour, didn't sit well with his doubling the price of drink for the night. After a few minutes of blabber the speaker introduced the second man as the promoter, a short-ass fellow with a shock of red hair. Even though the paying crowds had all been hauled in, he still spoke the sweet-talk of a snake-oil salesman drumming up trade.

Eventually the two men retreated and the boxing commenced, the beginning of the evening being taken up with preliminary bouts: local no-talent battlers trying to beat each other's brains out for a pittance.

When the warm-ups were over a swamper came in to clean the blood from the boards while the two suited men returned to announce the main bout of the evening. Then to the accompaniment of boos, Killer Garfield and his entourage made their entrance. Following a brief lull the crowd erupted in cheers as Big John strode in from the other side.

In long-legged tight-fitting drawers, the pugilists ducked in turn through the ropes and raised their arms in acknowledgement.

As Big John came to the front ropes he caught sight of JJ and clapped his hefty gloves in his direction. He didn't have quite the poundage of his opponent but he looked the fitter of the two. And, having seen him in action before, JJ had every faith in his friend.

Eventually the referee called the two men to the middle of the ring. 'The fight will be conducted according to the recently established London code,' he announced in a loud voice, 'otherwise known as the

Marquis of Queensberry rules.'

The men retired to their corners in preparation.

Then the bell clanged and the two pugilists came out. They circled each other warily, with Big John adopting the classic fists-up stance while his opponent moved his arms threateningly like some lumberjack in a saloon brawl. Suddenly the out-of-towner hurled himself forward swinging his huge, iron-like fists. Big John stepped nimbly aside and met him with a right that flattened the man's lip against his teeth. The fellow staggered back with blood gouting from the cut.

Blinking, he now threw himself at Big John once more, only to receive a blow to the side of his head for his effort. The blacksmith stayed in the centre of the ring, maintaining his stance, sidestepping every charge. Then, when the opportunity arose, his own fists worked in and out, with staggering force and dexterity. Time and time again he found his target, punishing the man's face and ribs with fists of fifteen inches circumference that packed the full power of his six-foot frame.

The first round continued in like fashion with the outsider rarely landing a punch, and it finished with Big John landing an explosive uppercut on the bell.

The visitor reeled from the blow, then staggered back to fall onto the stool in his corner where his seconds attempted to staunch the blood oozing from the mangled face. JJ smiled to himself. After all the hype and shouting of the odds, from the start the thing was little more than a one-sided contest.

He was musing that such is the way of these things when he suddenly became worried. As the bell rang for the second round, Big John looked in trouble. He came from his corner shaking his head as though recovering from a head blow, but he'd hardly been hit. JJ couldn't understand it. His lumbering, relatively unskilled opponent had hardly landed a punch during the whole of the first round.

But this time it was much different. There was no preliminary circling. Killer just rushed at him and Big John seemed incapable of doing anything other that going into a dazed, covering-up mode.

He rocked this way and that as the visitor thumped into him, like the out-of-towner was intent on delivering all the pain he could inflict on the town's golden boy. Big John went down under the onslaught and his opponent had to be dragged off him by the referee.

He beat the count but JJ could tell his friend didn't know where he was. Big John wavered on his feet for a moment before the man ran at him again, his attacker's arms less like flesh and blood, more resembling steam hammers, iron slamming into flesh and bone.

Big John began to crumple once more and a formidable right put him to the boards like a dead weight. But this time the referee didn't intervene as the man fisted and kicked the downed man.

As far as JJ could see, his friend was out. He leapt up and squeezed through the ropes.

'What's happened to the Marquis of Queensberry?' he yelled, as he put himself in between the unconscious Big John and his attacker. Eventually he managed to stave off Killer who began to strut round the ring with raised hands.

A second ran in with a bucket and threw water over Big John's face as the assembly erupted in boos, in part because the local man had lost and in part because their man didn't seem to have put up a proper fight. Someone shouted, 'If he had guts he left them in the dressing-room!'

When Big John's eyes opened, JJ helped the seconds to get him through to the back room which had been allocated as a dressing-room.

The hangers-on left as soon as the boxer had been dumped on a sofa and there was only the two of them.

'What happened?' JJ asked, when his friend had made some recovery.

'Dunno. Just went weak.'

'Did he catch you with some blow that I didn't see in the first round?'

Big John shook his head as he recalled events. 'Did he hell! Didn't touch me.'

'Well, something happened. You were a different man when you came out for the second round.'

He handed the boxer a towel. 'Let's get you cleaned up and back home.'

Later, when they were ensconced in Big John's living quarters in the smithy, JJ looked at the battered features of his friend. 'It sure is a hell of a way to earn your dough.'

'What dough?' Big John said, with a groan as he ran his fingers round his jaw. 'Don't collect a red cent. It was a winner-takes-all deal.'

JJ's eyebrows rose. 'What? You get nothing for your time? All that training and waltzing round the county promoting?'

Big John shook his head. 'It was in the contract.'

'Hell, John, didn't you read the small print?'

The boxer chuckled. 'With me not knowing my letters, JJ, I couldn't read the large print, never mind the small.'

They remained quiet for a while, then the boxer said in a low voice, 'I let the town down. All the folks I know and respect.'

'No, you didn't. Your manager let *you* down. I noticed he and the others in your team vamoosed once we'd got you out the ring. Through hell or high water, they should have stayed with you.' He pondered on the night's events. 'Tell you what: from where I was sitting, it had all the hallmarks of a fix. Some galoot slipped you a drop of something to slow you down.'

'Don't see how.'

'Your manager screwed you on the contract. That's plain. And he didn't fulfil his responsibility to protect you from somebody slipping you a Mickey Finn.' He thought about it some more. 'Fact is, I wouldn't put it past him to have been in on it. The promoter too.'

'No, they wouldn't.'

'Big John, they're all out for what they can get. The fight game's always been a honey pot for no-goods: prize-fighting, bare-knuckle scrapping. That's why authorities around the country are trying to bring some order to the business with the Queensberry rules and banning crude prize-fighting and such. But the muckamucks are still greasy snake-oilers, like all of the bigwigs there.

'Like the others, your manager probably had a big bucks bet against you himself. With you the favourite, a hefty bet on what he knew was a cert would have topped up his take with a handsome stash. And him being involved in the double-dealing would explain why he dropped you like a hot potato as soon as the thing was over. A good manager would have stayed to commiserate. Through thick and thin, as they say.'

He pondered on it. 'You have anything to

drink before the fight?'

'Yeah. A drink of water.'

'You normally have a drink immediately before a fight?'

'No. Don't want anything that'll bloat the stomach.'

'I didn't think so. You're experienced enough to know not to take any food or liquid in the close run-up to a bout.'

'No, I don't, not usually. But, funny thing is, I had a hell of a thirst tonight.'

'Who brought you the drink of water before the fight?'

'The Trask's houseboy.'

'When was the last time you ate?'

'Had my usual steaks around noon.'

'Salted?'

'Don't normally use much salt. But funny, now you mention it, they did taste kinda salty.'

JJ nodded. 'I figure that's how they did it. Where did you eat?'

'The restaurant over the road. The owner there laid on a free meal for me in line with the promotion.'

'Many there?'

'The place was full.'

'So anybody could have laden your beef with salt.'

'Yeah, 'spose so.'

'So that's how it was done. Got salt into your system which in time would make you thirsty so you break your habit and take a drink immediately before the fight; a drink with something in it but delivered by an innocent houseboy so there's no suspicion.'

He lit a cigar. 'Mind, we can't prove anything. Even if we could, there's so many bigwigs involved there's nothing we could do about it.' He shrugged. 'Big John, you'll just have to put this thing down to experience.'

They remained quiet for a while, JJ having said his piece and the boxer still a little woozy. After a while, JJ yawned and stood up to leave. 'We both need our rest tonight, pal.'

'Thanks for coming and for your support, JJ.'

JJ's expression changed. 'Say, I'd plumb forgot. Much as I was glad to turn up and help out, that wasn't the main reason for me showing my face. I'd gone over to the smithy to ask you something but hadn't realized the fight was tonight.'

'What did you want to know?'

'You seem to know the comings and goings in town, I wanted to ask if you knew anything about Ham Johnson.'

Eyes glazed, Big John tried to focus his thoughts and shook his head. But he managed to get some grip on his mental process, then said, 'Yeah, it's coming back to me. Funny you should ask, he appeared out of the blue yesterday while I was training. Hadn't seen him in a coon's age.'

'Nobody has. He's been holed up in Laramie Pen for a spell.'

'Yeah, I know. The bank heist a few years back.'

'He want anything special?'

'Yeah, wanted to know the where-at of a feller called Josh Arnold. Told him I didn't know the guy but thought he was maybe over at the Sullivan Hotel.'

JJ thought on it. 'OK, thanks,' he said slowly. 'Be seeing you.'

He stepped into the dimness of the street and headed along the boardwalk towards the guest house. So Johnson was in Julesburg.

Mere minutes after JJ had gone there came a knock at the smith's door. It was Ham Johnson. 'Heard about the fight, kid. Sorry the way it turned out.'

Big John shrugged. His mind was clearing. 'You win some, lose some.'

Johnson nodded at the door. 'The tall guy I spotted leaving. Who's he?'

Big John didn't like the question but it was only with great effort he could get his scrambled brains round to deflecting it. 'Er ... er ... just some punter come to give his commiserations.'

'I gather Red Crawford promoted the fight.'

'Yeah. He fronted a syndicate up at the Lodge that set up the thing.'

'This Lodge place, you a member?'

Big John chuckled. 'You're kidding. Only top brass are members of that joint.'

'But, their setting up the fight, they'd know you.'

'Sure. Even went in as a guest a couple of times.'

'So you'd have no problem getting in again.'

The blacksmith grunted. 'After my performance tonight, I don't think so.'

'But they know you. You've been in before. You could get in again on some pretext.'

Big John considered the notion. 'Maybe, if I had to.'

'OK, I want you to get me in. Quiet like.'

The boxer shook his weary head. 'I don't know if I could do that, Ham.'

'It's worth fifty dollars.'

'Ain't denying I can use the money,' Big John said. He mulled over the possibilities. 'Come to think of it, there's a side door.

Always locked as far as I know. Never seen it used. I suppose, if I could get to it, I could slip the inside bolt, if it's that important.'

Johnson took out the bills and handed them across. 'It's important.'

'When?' the pugilist asked.

'I was thinking of tonight.'

'Jeez, I'm bushed, Ham. I've had helluva night.'

Johnson peeled off some more bills and threw them across.

Big John looked at them added them to the pile and counted the total. 'OK, but you don't tell Crawford it was me let you in.'

Johnson winked. 'Of course not.'

'Just give me time to clean up.'

'Now tell me about the layout inside,' Johnson said a few minutes later, as they headed for the door. 'And where Crawford is likely to be in there.'

EIGHT

Deputy Dink Talbot was irritated. It rankled him that his boss had recommended an outsider to Archie Royal. He would have relished the chance of facing up to Ham Johnson himself. Dropping the renegade would get him into the papers, give him a much needed rep. Maybe give him the clout to move on. The world was bigger than a one-horse town like Julesburg. Not to mention there was a good chance the wealthy Royal would throw some money his way for solving his problem.

He sat alone in the law office thinking on these matters. It was his shift and, with the fight at the Trask Hotel finishing early, the excitement over and drunks were already on their way home, it was turning into another quiet night. Full of nervous tension he stood up and practised drawing. Yeah, he could take Johnson on, no problem. Why did his boss have to recommend an old fogy?

He found the Johnson poster in his boss's desk. He studied the picture for some time, familiarized himself with the features, then returned it to the drawer.

Yes, sir, it would be a real feather in his cap if he could nail Johnson before Washington did. But where would he find him? As far as he knew, Johnson had no kin in town. He didn't know Red Crawford very well but knew he was one of the town's kingpins and as such should have his finger on the pulse of the locality. Nothing like starting at the top. Crawford might know Johnson's whereat.

And Dink knew where to find him. The Lodge, the imposing building on the edge of town. Set up by Crawford it was the local headquarters of the Grand Order of Teutonic Knights, one of the many societies that had been brought over from Europe. It was whispered they conducted strange initiation ceremonies. The story went that it was supposed to be something to do with old-time chivalry but, apart from being linked to the Klan, everyone knew it really existed to serve the self-interests of its members. Made up of local tradesmen and bureaucrats, not to mention every crook in town, its *raison d'être* was bound to be about making money.

Trouble was the place was strictly barred to outsiders. But maybe if he watched the place...

As a lawman on official business he might even gain entrance. He'd always wanted to see the inside of the mysterious place. He stood up, checked the set of his gun on his hips. Yes, he'd include it in his rounds this very night.

He had done his usual circuit of the town by the time he knocked at the door of the enigmatic building. At first there was no answer and he guessed it was normally only opened following a secret knock. But he persevered, his banging getting louder. Eventually it was opened, just enough for him to see a rough, scarred face.

'What d'you want?' the mouth in the face growled.

'I want to come in and speak to Mr Crawford.'

The door opened slightly more and he could see the face was perched on a thick-set body, while a figure of similar proportions stood behind him. 'There's no way you're coming in, mister,' the man said. 'Members only. Now beat it.'

'I'm the law and if you carry on like this I'm gonna fetch back-up and we'll smash our way in.'

It was a bluff but it worked. The man looked at his comrade who nodded, and Dink was shown inside.

'Stay here,' the doorman said. 'I'll have a word with Mr Crawford and see what he has to say.' The man left him under the watchful eye of the second man. The lobby was darkly lit, the low oil-lamps cast ominous shadows while adding highlights to the polished, ornately carved panelling. Even in the relative darkness Dink could see the eye watching him was a mean and threatening one.

'What is this?' Crawford said, when he eventually emerged from an inner door. He was short, his grey hair dyed a lurid red. He bowed stiffly from the waist as he walked.

'Deputy Dink Talbot, Mr Crawford. I'm looking for Ham Johnson and have reason to believe you might know his where-at.'

'Well, your reasoning is wrong, Mr Deputy. The only Johnson I know of is pissing in a bucket out at Laramie Pen.'

'Well, he's out of the can and headed this way. We thought you, as one the important figures in town, might have some idea.'

'Like I said, you thought wrong. Now, if you'll excuse me.' And he disappeared back through the door, throwing a nod to the two doormen. 'See the gentleman out.'

Back in the street, Dink felt even more disgruntled, seeing himself as having been treated like a no-account kid. He stood in the shadows and built himself a smoke in an attempt to combat his frustration.

He was about to make his way back into town, when he saw two figures approaching. They were two big men.

Even though they were some distance away and it was dark he recognized one, simply by his frame and gait: Big John McBride, the blacksmith. But the other was unfamiliar to him.

They stopped, exchanged a few low-voiced words and McBride pointed to the side of the building. Then he went round to the front while the second man remained in the shadows. McBride knocked at the door and was allowed entry.

Minutes passed and the man in the darkness didn't move. Dink was intrigued. What was going on? He remained still, biding his time. Eventually McBride came out of the building. When he got level with the man he didn't speak but pointed enigmatically to the side and carried on back into town.

The man emerged from the darkness and headed for the side of the building in the direction that Big John had indicated. Only the light of the moon was available but Dink could see enough to recognize the face. It had the features he had seen on the poster in the law office file: Ham Johnson.

He waited until Johnson had disappeared around the corner, then he approached the building and positioned himself against the wall at the corner. He peered round. The alley was empty. He moved stealthily down the passage and came across a door. It was clear that this was the means by which the man had gained access. However, when Dink examined it, he could find no handle. He pushed quietly and firmly, but it refused to budge. The door had been opened for Johnson from the inside – probably by Big John – then locked again. But why the clandestine means of entry? Was this where Johnson was holing up? He pondered on his next move.

Inside, Johnson allowed his eyes to acclimatize to the relative darkness, then moved slowly along the corridor. Thanks to the description he had been given by the blacksmith he had an idea of the layout, knew that halfway along the corridor there were stairs. He reached them and mounted slowly, keeping away from the centre of the wooden steps to minimize creaks.

At the top he gripped the banister and eased himself onto the landing. From that point on he didn't have to concern himself with the sound of his footfalls as the corridor on higher floor was carpeted. He noted the room that would be Crawford's. A slit of light ran along the foot of the door.

He stepped gingerly along the corridor and turned off the solitary oil lamp on the wall. Guided by the strip of light, he approached the door. He drew his gun, took a firm hold of the knob and stepped smartly in.

Crawford was seated at a desk, poring over some papers. He couldn't mask the amazement in his eyes when he looked up. 'Ham!' he spluttered. 'I thought you ... you ... were in the pen.'

'No, you didn't. You knew I was out. But I can understand your surprise in seeing me,'

'Well, good to see you, pal. How you doing?'

'Better than you intended me to be.'

'What do you mean?'

'You know what I mean.'

'Hey, this deserves a drink,' Crawford said, extending an arm towards a bottle at the end of his desk.

'No it don't. Leave that hand where it is, where I can see it, and don't make any more moves like that.'

Crawford looked puzzled. 'Why the gun, Ham?'

'You know the why of that too. You tried to plant me.'

'Dunno what you're talking about.'

'But before I do anything about it, I want to know why you paid good money to see me fitted for a pine box.'

The seated man ran a sweat-sticky palm over his red hair. 'Do anything about it? What the hell are you talking about, Ham?'

'You paid some guys to jump me. And they weren't trying to scare me off. They wasn't fooling. It had all the looks of a contract job. And, as you can see by the fact I'm standing here, the stunt didn't come off. In fact, it's them that's pushing up daisies.' He chuckled. 'Josh Arnold too.'

Crawford's eyes narrowed. 'Josh Arnold? So that was you.' Too late, he realized he'd spluttered out the words impulsively.

'Yeah,' Johnson said, nodding at the implication. 'But never mind that.' He moved across the room to a spot from whence he could cover the door, and he dropped onto a chair. 'Fact is, I can't see any reason for you organizing this business. The way I see it, we've always got along. Leastwise, after a fashion. There's no money at stake. We all got our cuts. I ain't never harmed you and I got nothing against you. I just can't get my head round the whys and wherefores of you paying somebody to plant me.'

'I still don't know what this is all about. The whole thing's got me beat too, Ham. Must be crossed wires somewheres. We're buddies, as you say.'

Johnson grunted in frustration and stood up. 'I can see you're just gonna keep stonewalling me. Ain't no point in continuing this discussion. You ain't gonna admit anything outright or explain. But you've said enough.' His voice dropped to determined grunt. 'So, nothing left but payback time.' He crossed to a plush *chaise-longue* nearer the desk and, keeping his gun level, picked up one of the cushions. 'Sorry, it's ending this way, Red.'

'No, Ham. Don't be crazy.'

Johnson stepped around the desk. He was just raising the cushion to cover the muzzle of his gun when there was the clump of feet outside. He heard muffled tones:

'It's me: Leroy.' And the door swung open to reveal one of Crawford's henchmen.

'That damn lawman's back, boss...' the

man said, before he caught sight of Johnson's gun. 'What the hell's going on?' he snapped, his hand diving to the inside of his jacket for his own weapon.

Johnson swung the cushion at the lamp on the wall. There was the crash of shattering glass and guns barked in the ensuing blackness.

After seconds of unseen turmoil and further gunfire, the door crashed open.

'Get him!' Crawford yelled.

'I'm hit, boss.'

'Get the bastard!' Crawford shouted, as he scrabbled in the darkness through his desk in search of a gun.

The henchman staggered outside the room. In the murk he saw a figure silhouetted at the end of the passage and he fired. Seconds later, Crawford joined him and advanced towards the downed man. He turned the figure over and through the gloom could see the faint glint of a badge. 'Congratulations, Leroy. You've killed yourself a lawman.'

He leapt up and ran across the landing yelling for his men. 'You guys, get Johnson. The critter's in the place somewhere.'

Minutes on, the search revealed nothing. Back on the landing with a lantern in his hand, he looked down at the dead man. Now he could clearly see the face. 'It's the deputy, Talbot.'

Leroy was leaning against the wall, holding his side. 'What we gonna do about him, boss?'

Crawford kicked the thing round his mind for a moment. 'No problem. The way we tell it: Talbot came here asking after Johnson but we couldn't help him. We'll dump the body in town in an out-of-the way spot and rig it so it looks like a shootout. Won't be difficult to provide a witness.'

He smiled in satisfaction. 'That'll put us in the clear – plus Johnson's gunning down a lawman gives us a legitimate reason to kill him.'

More men joined them.

'So,' he continued, 'three of you stay here

with me. You others get out there, find Johnson. He can't have got far. And put paid to the bozo; once and for all.'

Out in the gloom of the night he instructed one of the remaining men to scout ahead, ensuring the coast was clear and the body of the young deputy was carried along the back alley that ran parallel with the main drag. When they came to an isolated spot, Crawford halted the party.

'OK,' he said. 'Seth, you stay here. Everybody else get home and hit the sack like nothing has happened.'

Seth Coolidge was the oldest member of the crew. With few teeth left in his head and a mite doddery, he was only kept on because of his being a distant cousin of Red's. Except for running messages, the fellow was next to useless but occasionally he had some purpose. Like now.

When they were alone, Crawford turned to him. 'Seth, you hightail it back to the Lodge and leave the side door unlocked for me.' He hung back a few minutes to give the oldster time to get clear, then he took Dink's gun from its holster and fired it into the night air. He placed the gun in the deputy's hand, fired another round skyward from his own gun and then headed for the Lodge.

Minutes later he came down the stairs from his office with a bottle of whiskey in his hand. 'Now, Seth, shuck your gunbelt. Take a few swigs of this, keep the bottle in your hand and go knocking on the sheriff's door. Tell him you saw Johnson shoot Talbot. You've had a rep for the booze ever since I was a kid. So act like you been out all night hitting the stuff. You've been known to do that before. Can you do that? And stick to the story. You happened upon the two of them standing face-to-face having some argument. Then Johnson pumped him full of lead.'

Seth nodded, did as he was bid, his eyes unfalteringly fixed on the bottle.

Crawford took out a billfold and stuffed a handful of paper into the man's pocket. 'And keep away from the Lodge for a spell.'

NINE

There was a crowd round the law office when JJ stepped out onto the street the next morning. He worked his way through the onlookers.

'Ham Johnson's in town all right,' the sheriff said when JJ joined him. 'He gunned down my deputy. Seems Dink caught up with him and there was a shootout.'

'Any idea which way he went?'

'No. The old fellow who saw it, a local jughead, had been out on a bender and was seven seas over.'

'Your only witness is a drunk? Is that reliable evidence?'

'Got nothing else. I've been round asking a few questions but it's like looking for a needle in a haystack. Some folks heard the shots but nobody else saw anything. It was very late. Anyways, I've managed to enrol a couple of special deputies. They're out now asking folks if they saw or heard anything.'

'Where did it happen?'

The sheriff explained the location and JJ went to cast his eye over the scene. But the ground was solid-packed earth and even the experienced eye of a one-time bounty hunter couldn't pick up any clues.

When he got back to the law office the sheriff pushed a piece of paper across the desk. 'You might be interested in that. It's just come in.'

JJ picked it up. It was a telegraph message from the Albany County law office. He cast his eye over the content. It told of two men found dead on the trail. A railroad surveyor had heard gunfire and investigated. He reported what he had seen back at his base at Tie Siding. And that there had been a man riding away. He hadn't been able to get a close look but the man was riding a grey with what looked like a white flash. The base had passed the information to the civilian law office.

'Why would I be interested?'

'This is a quiet county. Here in town, for example, last night's shooting was the first time we've had guns fired in earnest since the bank heist over three years ago. We don't get much hard violence. Then madman Johnson gets released and there are three dead.' He nodded to the map on the wall. 'Tie Siding is on the trail between Laramie and here. In addition, the witness saw the guy riding off to the north – in this direction. Looks like this thing could develop into our business.'

JJ nodded. 'So we'd like to know if Johnson's riding a white-flashed grey.'

'It would be interesting to know,' the sheriff said, but then made a dismissive gesture. 'On the other hand, the trail from Laramie is not my territory. Anyways, for the moment it's a secondary matter to me. I'm more concerned to nail Johnson for killing Dink.'

'These dead men out near Tie Siding –

what do you think happened?'

'Maybe a couple of saddlebums aiming to rob a lone rider, not knowing what kind of man they were jumping. But the way the guy put 'em out of action points strongly to the likelihood of it being our man. Dry-gulchers picking on the wrong guy.'

'Opportunist saddlebums,' JJ conceded. 'Or somebody was deliberately aiming to knock him off for some reason.'

Outside, JJ lit a cheroot and leaned on the rail. The sheriff had said three had been killed in the short time that Johnson had been out. But not long after the former bounty hunter had ridden into town he had learned of a man falling from a hotel balcony. Apparently it had been an accident. That's what had gone down in the record but, if it hadn't been an accident, that would make *four* who had been killed since Johnson's release.

He cast his mind back to the accident the mortician spoke of. The deceased's name had been Josh Arnold and he had been staying at the Sullivan Hotel. Might be worth some investigation.

The proprietor of the Sullivan was preoccupied with a newspaper when JJ walked in. The man pasted on a false smile, which disappeared when he realized the caller was not in the market for one of his rooms; and he returned to his reading after JJ's question.

'I asked you what you can tell me about this Josh Arnold who was staying here,' JJ repeated.

'Not much,' the man said, without looking up from his paper. 'Like I told the sheriff after the accident, he was a businessman passing through. Polite feller. Bit of a German accent, maybe. That's about it.'

'There's nothing else you can tell me?'

'Listen, mister, are you law?'

'Kind of.'

'What's that mean? I don't see no badge.'

JJ's left hand gestured vaguely in the

direction of law office. 'It means you can check my credentials with Sheriff Connor.' But a fraction later his demeanour changed and his voice brittled with a hard animosity. 'But we don't want to waste each other's time, do we, my friend?'

He noted how the man dragged the back of his hand across his mouth. His mouth was going dry.

'Now I want answers to questions,' JJ continued.

'I just aim to keep my nose clean, mister.'

'You might get it broken if you keep this up. Now, answers. Like, how come a fit and capable man just falls over a balcony rail?'

'It was an accident, mister. That's what the coroner said.'

'Did anyone witness it?'

'No.'

'So, it's just supposition that it was an accident.'

'What else could it be?'

'Let's have a look at the scene. So if you'll show me...'

The man instructed an underling to watch the desk and led JJ outside. At the back he pointed to the stairs and balcony. With a sweep of his hand, indicated the trajectory of the fall.

'Well, let's consider the run-up to the so-called accident.'

'What's that mean?'

'It means: anything untoward happen, prior to the incident?'

'Such as?'

'Such as – you tell me.'

The man shrugged. 'There's nothing to tell, mister. First thing I knew was folks coming in to tell me there had been an unfortunate mishap out here.' He had tried to make his movement casual, but JJ could detect some concern in the man's eyes.

'You've been threatened, ain't you?'

'I'm just trying to run a hotel here, mister. None of this is my affair.'

'The man was killed on your premises. That's makes it your affair. Come on. Let's see if we can get some more perspective from up on the balcony.'

At the top he asked which had been Arnold's room.

The man showed him. JJ walked the length of the walkway, inspecting the windows. 'You don't clean the windows very often, do you?'

'Maybe once a month. What's that got to do with it?'

'The dust on the other windows is undisturbed, inside and out. Yet there are fingerprints on both sides of the glass on Arnold's window. Was his window open at the time of the accident?'

'Yes.'

'His door locked from the inside?'

'Yes.'

'He doing a runner?'

'Maybe.'

'Or maybe somebody was after him. Now, who was it?'

'I don't earn enough from this place as it is, mister. I–'

'I'm here for answers,' JJ butted in, 'not a

catechism of complaints. We've all got our problems. And at the moment my problem is you.' He looked down at the ground. 'Seems to me a guy could fall from here without getting hisself killed.' He stepped back to the wall. 'What do you think?'

'Dunno. If he fell wrong...'

Suddenly JJ pulled his gun, grabbed the man's shoulder and pushed him against the rail. 'Of course, for the purposes of our enquiry we could try a little experiment.' His gun was jabbed hard in the man's stomach. 'Do you think you could make it to the ground and live? I think you've got a chance of surviving.'

The man's eyes rolled. 'What are you doing?'

'I've told you – pursuing an investigation in the name of the law. Now, he was running all right – but from somebody, not the hotel check. Somebody was at his door; or had passed word he was downstairs waiting. OK, who came in just prior?'

'You won't tell nobody?' the man faltered.

'No. Now stop beating around the grease-wood and spill it out.'

'Says his name was Mr Laramie. Came asking after Josh Arnold. Then went out the front, told me to leave it a few minutes then go to Mr Arnold's room and tell him Mr Laramie was waiting downstairs. That's all I know.'

JJ nodded. 'That few minutes – that would be long enough for this Laramie fellow to get round to the balcony?'

'Reckon so.'

JJ nodded and headed for the steps. 'You've been mighty obliging,' he said, the tension dissolving from his voice. 'Now be careful coming down. These steps seems a mite rickety.'

His next stop was the smithy.

'You remember you told me Ham Johnson came asking if you knew the where-at of Josh Arnold?' he began.

Big John nodded. 'Yeah.'

JJ studied his friend's face, saw no

reaction. 'Then you haven't heard?'

'Heard what?'

'Arnold fell from the hotel balcony shortly afterwards.'

'And you think it was Johnson?'

'Well nobody saw anything, but I reckon so. A fellow calling hisself Mr Laramie was the last one to see Arnold alive. Immediately before the so-called accident. I reckon the name Laramie was being used because it would mean something to Arnold.'

The blacksmith leant against the wall, his eyes rolling up to the rafters. 'Laramie... Johnson had just come out of Laramie Pen. Jeez, and I told him where the guy was.'

'Don't blame yourself, Johnny. You had no means of knowing. More important, you got any idea where Johnson is now?'

'No, but he came again to see me after you left. Asked me to help getting him into the Lodge.'

'The Lodge?'

'Place at the end of town. Some kind of society of local bigwigs.'

'Why did he want to go there?'

'Had some business with Red Crawford. He's the big wheel there.'

TEN

He returned to the law office.

'This guy who fell off the balcony,' he said to the sheriff, 'you get a good look at the body?'

'Yeah.'

'Anything familiar about him?'

'No. He was a stranger in town. The hotel proprietor said he was some businessman passing through.'

JJ thought for a moment, then had an idea. 'You're a methodical man, Lee. You still keep your old dodgers like you used to?'

'Yeah. Old habits die hard. Keep some in the drawer here. Others are gathering dust in a card-box somewheres in the storeroom.'

'Do me a favour and have a look through 'em for me, will you? See if you recognize a face. Just a long shot.'

'Don't see the point, but if you say so.'

Minutes later he was seated at his desk, working through a stack of reward posters, with JJ looking over his shoulder.

He'd got almost to the end when he paused and went back to an earlier one. 'Well, I'll be...' He angled this way and that to change his perspective, then pointed to the daguerreotype features. 'I don't have to tell you how unfaithful these so-called likenesses can be, but on closer scrutiny this fellow could bear something of a resemblance to the recently deceased Mr Arnold.'

JJ read the legend. The charge was SUSPECTED CONSPIRACY TO MURDER. The name Arnold wasn't there but there was a long list of aliases. He gave a grunt of realization and pointed to one of them. 'The Dutchman,' he read out loud with some satisfaction and added, 'You ever notice how a Dutch accent sounds like a

German one?'

The sheriff shrugged. 'Can't say I have. Spent all my life out here in the back of nowhere. So ain't ever heard a German or a Dutchman. What's the point?'

'The guy at the Sullivan said Arnold had a faint German accent.'

The sheriff nodded. 'Interesting.'

'I'll tell you something else just as interesting: the name Dutchman came up a lot in my line of work.'

'In what way?'

'There was guy they called the Dutchman. Acted as a middleman, a fixer. Worked out of Chicago but travelled all over. One or two *hombres* I got bounties on mentioned him as being in back of things. But no law agency could get anything on him that would stick. That's why the word "suspected" is on the dodger.'

'What was his line?'

'If you wanted somebody putting out of the way but didn't want to dirty your hands you called him in. Provided you had money, that is. He came expensive. A sight more than thirty a month and found.'

The sheriff shook his head in disbelief. 'This Arnold guy, he was a mild-looking feller. Didn't look like a paid killer.'

'He wasn't. His method was to pay others to do the job. He was an organizer. He knew every coyote capable of murder from Yuma to El Paso. That way there was no direct connection between those who wanted the job doing and the victim.'

'You think he was here in town to arrange a job?'

'Maybe. Or maybe the job had already been done.' He thought on it, remembered the corpses out near Tie Siding and added, 'Or attempted.'

He called in at the Sullivan Hotel once more. This time he received the prompt attention of its proprietor. The man was taking the details of some new lady guests but the moment he caught sight of JJ's frame in the door, he promptly put down his pen. 'Excuse me, ladies. Yes, sir. What can I do for you?'

'One more question. You know of any contacts this Arnold had while he was in town?'

The man shook his head. 'Didn't go out much at all. And only had one caller, as I recall. Mr Crawford from the Lodge. He spent some time with Mr Arnold up in his room.'

JJ stepped out onto the boardwalk. Crawford. There was that name again.

JJ was missing his Em. And her cooking. He pondered on it. If he returned home for the night he could visit the Crown Ranch in the morning on his way back to Julesburg. Besides, there was a guy by the name of Alamo in Dry Gulch who might prove interesting to talk to at this juncture.

He checked out of the guest house and headed north. As he neared Dry Gulch he pushed his mount into a long lope. At the outskirts of town he slowed to a walk and reined in at a shack.

A young girl greeted him at the door. 'Why, Mr Washington. Good to see you.'

'Likewise, miss.'

'What can I do for you?'

'Your pa in?'

'No. I wheel him over to the saloon in the afternoon. Helps to pass the time.'

He touched his hat. 'Thanks.'

Alamo, the girl's father, was a one-time owlhoot and had crossed trails with JJ on more than one occasion. The last time, some ten years since, Alamo had been involved in a payroll robbery at a local lumber company. During the chase Alamo had fallen and broken a leg. The wound turned gangrenous and the limb had had to be amputated. Reckoning the guy had been punished enough, JJ made no mention of him in his report and had sought prosecution only of Alamo's confederates.

He made his way into town and pulled in at the saloon. Early evening, there was only one customer: a guy in a wheelchair.

Alamo pumped JJ's hand, enjoying the sight of his old adversary, and looked the visitor up and down. 'Hey, what's happened to your storekeeper's coat?'

JJ shifted the buckskin jacket enough to reveal one of his guns.

Alamo nodded. 'Back in the old job, eh?'

JJ shrugged. 'Kind of. Just for a short while.' He gestured to the bar. 'What you having?'

'Another beer if you're paying. Thank you kindly.'

'Let's take 'em out on the porch,' JJ said, as he collected a couple of foaming glasses. 'It'll give us a chance to catch some of the afternoon sun afore it disappears.'

'Your health,' Alamo said, raising his glass to his lips after he had been wheeled outside. 'I won't hear a word against you, Mr Washington. Heart as big as a barn door.'

For a while they exchanged small talk, then JJ said, 'Tell me, you still keep your ear close to the ground?' He knew the man did, but he asked the question as a way of broaching the subject.

Curiosity burned in the other's eyes. 'I suppose you could say so. Why?'

'Bank heist in Julesburg some three years ago. Big job, hit all the papers. There were three involved. Ham Johnson who did time for it, and two others, unknowns. One died from a gunshot but another got away. Any idea who?'

The other shook his head. 'Afraid not. Anyways, much as I got respect for you, Mr Washington, you know I ain't no stoolie.'

The veteran manhunter studied the face, read what was happening behind the eyes. 'Of course. But if you did know and told me, you wouldn't be breaking any code. I'm not wearing a badge no more, so I ain't after the fellow to nail him for the job. Fact is, I'm trying to put together a bit of a puzzle. If I knew who the guy was it might help to explain a few things.'

Alamo paused, then something of a smile crinkled his leathery face. 'You've always been straight with me, Mr Washington. I'll take you at your word.' He looked up and down the street and continued in lowered tones. 'The whisper was it was Red Crawford. Fact is, I never like the bastard. Double-crossed me once in the old days.'

JJ nodded. Things were fitting.

Alamo chuckled. 'When he was younger the jasper had this big shock of red hair. He was so proud of it. Combing it all the time. Then it turned grey prematurely. But folks still called him Red.'

'Well, it's red again. Real red.'

'He dyeing it?'

'And some. He looks like a saloon doxie!'

Alamo's chuckle became a guffaw. 'The pathetic, vain bastard.'

JJ sipped his drink. 'There's a place called the Lodge in Huntsville. Grand place on the edge of town. Crawford's got something to do with it. You know anything about the place?'

'Only a whisper. Some kind of front, so it's said. Dunno what they're up to in there but you can bet it's something nefarious with

Crawford involved. Let's say I know Crawford ain't retired.'

JJ bought another drink and they continued with their chitchat for a while.

Finally as he rose to leave, Alamo grabbed his hand. 'I don't know what you're planning, store-man, but you be careful. Ain't many crossed Red and lived.'

JJ winked and stuffed a bill in the other's pocket. 'Thanks. Good seeing you, Alamo.'

'Afore you go, wheel me back inside. I've had enough of the great outdoors for one day.'

After a slap-up home-cooked meal, JJ crawled into bed, wrapped his beloved Em in his arms and dropped off to sleep.

On his way back to Julesburg the following day, he stopped by the Crown Ranch.

'How are things developing?' Royal wanted to know, when they met on the veranda of the ranch house.

'If Johnson did have you lined up in his sights – which I don't believe for a moment

– he ain't gonna be bothered anymore. He's got something more important than some supposed grudge on his mind now. He's wanted for killing a lawman, the deputy out at Julesburg.'

'Jeez. What's that all about?'

'Dunno, but with the law after him, you're going to be the last thing on his mind – if you were ever on it in the first place, which I doubt. Anyways, you don't need me here; you got enough protection. The best way is still for me to seek him out.'

'Any ideas?'

'Some things might be clicking into place.'

ELEVEN

In town he was heading along the boardwalk to the law office when something caught his eye. He wasn't even looking for it, but years of manhunting had ingrained into him an alertness that worked at the subconscious level.

Hitched alongside others outside a saloon was a chestnut – and part of its left ear was missing. He stopped, leant on the boardwalk rail and, with the air of someone with nothing to do, he looked casually up and down the street while simultaneously appraising the animal. Its flesh was scarred like it had fallen on barb-wire; or had taken more than its fair share of lashings from some black-hearted bastard who got some kick out of ill-treating dumb animals.

He turned, gave the saloon the once-over, then shoved through the batwing doors and walked to the bar. The place was loud with the collision of voices.

Simply nosing around would create suspicion so he eyed the beverages on offer. In his bachelor days, whiskey had been his penchant – a good malt, not the raw stuff common to most western saloons – but he hadn't indulged for a long, long time. No harm in mixing business with pleasure from time to time. He noted a dusty bottle on a top shelf, could make out the word malt on the label, and he ordered a shot.

While he savoured it he looked around the room taking the measure of its occupants. There was handful of lone drinkers and small groups. Up in a corner a game of acey-deucey was in progress while a couple of gangs of noisy drovers made up the rest of the clientele.

Taking advantage of the need to look as though he was simply there for leisure purposes, he took his cigar case from his pocket and extracted a cheroot. One of the benefits of running a store, he got classy cigars at cost price.

He lit up and strolled over to a table. He squinted through the smoke curling up from the end of his cigar. It wasn't long before he saw it. On the arm of one of the card players, the tattoo of a Confederate flag. Royal's foreman had mentioned such a tattoo. Of course, it could be coincidence. The Rebel flag was not an uncommon adornment. But the probabilities were stacking up.

In a manner designed not to show his intention, he took stock of the fellow, just listening and watching. Close-cropped hair, not much more than a kid. He'd seen the kind in a score of towns across the West. The type who thought he was the cock of the walk, too young yet to have met his comeuppance. Yet underneath the brashness, a coward at heart who undertook no action unless he had the upper hand, like having a gun in his hand, or sneaking up behind a guy. And the kind who would dish it out to some dumb animal tied to a post.

The banter around the table was liquor and its consumption. One of the men suddenly laughed as he placed a card on the table. He thumbed at the tattooed youngster. 'You know, Beaudine here was so squiffed a while back, he fell headfirst into the water trough at the end of the drag. The younker just can't handle his booze!'

'No I didn't,' the youngster snapped

stiffly, his eyes drink-bleared.

'Yes, you did. Remember, a month back?'

'Oh, yeah,' the lad conceded. 'But I didn't trip! I did it intentionally. I was just freshening up was all.'

The other speaker laughed. 'Yeah, like hogs can fly.'

The other players joined in the laughter to the chagrin of the tattooed young man.

So, JJ mused. The storyteller had said a month back. In that case the illustrated 'Rebel' hadn't been in the pen. If this Beaudine was the one who had bent Archie Royal's ear with a tale about Johnson seeking revenge – and all the signs pointed to that fact – he hadn't just been released from a stretch as he had claimed. So why had he ridden out to the Crown and spun a yarn to the ranch owner? Not a prank with any obvious return. Hadn't been done casually; had to be some deep reason, some plan, maybe. But the tattooed kid was too young and fond of his drink to dream up something complicated. If his going out to the

Crown and putting the scare into Archie Royal was part of some scheme, he had been working under orders. But orders from whom?

JJ took another drink while he continued listening to the banter but nothing useful was coming out of it and, when he realized the card game still had some mileage to go, he went outside and took occupancy in a boardwalk chair opposite the saloon.

In time the group emerged and mounted up. He waited until they were some distance along the drag and he followed.

His shadowing of them didn't take long. On the outskirts of town they pulled in at the building he now knew to be the Lodge. He drew rein some distance away and dismounted. Pretending to examine his horse's hoof, he watched them hitch their horses and disappear inside the building.

So, the young tattooed fellow who had masqueraded as an ex-con just out of the pen was part of the Crawford set-up.

Interesting. And what was that all about?

Maybe it was time to visit the famed Lodge. He led his horse back and tethered it to the first rail he came to. Then he strolled back to the Lodge and knocked on the door.

A burly man with a bandaged arm answered the door.

'The name's Washington. I'm working with Sheriff Connors. I'd like to speak with Mr Crawford.'

Eventually the man with the bright red hair he had seen at the boxing venue came to the door. He looked the visitor up and down. 'Washington?' he said. 'Don't know the name. You one of the special deputies the sheriff's taken on?'

'I'm working with him.'

'So what is it?'

'I'm wondering if you know the where-at of Ham Johnson.'

'Like I told your boss, how should I know?'

'I heard he came here just before the shooting.'

'Yeah, he did come a-knocking.'

'What did he want?'

'Don't know. He wasn't allowed in. He's not a member.'

'So you know nothing about his where-at?'

'That's the size of it. All I do know is sometime later there was gunfire and he'd gunned down the deputy. Rather than wasting my time you should be out looking for him.'

JJ touched his hat. 'Thank you for your time, sir.'

Big John was working up a sweat pounding a horseshoe on the anvil when JJ appeared at the door. 'You had some dealings with Johnson when he first came to town,' he said, when they had exchanged greetings. 'You know his horse?'

'No.'

'Pity.' Then: 'You know of any unfamiliar horses in town?'

The blacksmith thought on it. 'Now you mention it, there's one I didn't recognize over at Jim Taggart's livery. He's stabling an unfamiliar mount. A grey with white flash. I was over there this morning, fixing a shoe on one his own horses. Noticed the grey but had no reason to ask any questions. That's the only thing I can come up with, JJ.'

'Thanks. I'll check it out.'

'As you don't know Jim, just mention my name.'

Over at the livery, JJ introduced himself. A brief glance around the interior was enough for him to identify the grey with the white flash. He walked over to the horse. 'Classy bit of horseflesh,' he commented. 'Mind if I take a closer look?'

'Help yourself.'

Emitting soothing sounds, JJ entered the stall and stroked the animal to show he was no threat. 'Whose is it?'

'Don't know the feller. Just saw him the once when he booked the stall and paid up front.'

JJ examined each hoof in turn. 'Looks like it's been rid a long way.'

'Not far enough to need new shoes yet. I've checked.'

JJ patted the horse once again and came out of the stall. 'You know where this fellow's staying?'

The hostler stopped in his task and reappraised his visitor. 'You tell me you're a pal of Big John's, but you're asking a heap of questions. I gotta respect my customers. Besides, I ain't never heard of you.'

'You heard of Lee Connor?'

'Yeah. The sheriff.'

'Well, I'm working in association with him. If you're all that concerned about imparting customer confidences, check me out with him next time you see him. Him and me go back a long ways. Now I asked you if you knew where this guy's staying.'

'No.'

'You sure?'

'Yeah.'

'OK. And thanks for your trouble.'

He'd just got to the door when he heard the man's voice behind him. 'It's coming back to me. Slipped my mind. I have seen him before.'

JJ paused. 'Yeah?'

'I caught a glimpse of him the other day at the end of the street.'

'What was he doing out there?'

'Can't say. Ain't no stores or businesses out that far.'

JJ mused on the information. 'Is that Drovers' shack still out that a-ways?'

'Sure. Old Ma Cannon. She's still there. Always will be I reckon. Hell, she's gonna outlive us all.' He paused. 'But I don't think the guy who owns this horse would be staying there. He was dressed fair and clean-looking. Don't look like the kind who would be happy to share fleas with Ma's usual run of desert rats.'

'Unless he had reasons.'

'Besides, being no-accounts, not many of Ma's "guests" stretch to having a hoss. Those that do, tie 'em under the awning out back of her place. Saves 'em the cents they'd have to cough up for quartering 'em somewhere decent like here.'

Again, unless there's a reason, JJ thought. Some other reason why he hadn't wanted to leave his horse there. From what JJ remembered of the place the animals were tethered under a simple, open awning and could be seen from the street.

'Anything else you've just remembered?' he asked.

'No.'

'OK,' JJ said, stepping towards the sunlight. 'Do me one last favour. Don't tell him anybody was asking about him or his horse.'

'As you say, mister.'

He strolled through town until he got to The Drovers. Out back he found Old Ma Cannon sitting on a rocking chair, clicking knitting needles.

'Good day, ma'am,' he said, touching his hat brim. 'You got a pallet for a weary traveller?'

She looked him up and down and smiled. 'You don't look weary nor no traveller.' She continued looking him over with an enigmatic smile playing across her whang-leather face. 'Don't know what you're after, mister, but by the cut of them clothes it sure ain't one of my doss cots.'

'I take it the answer's no?'

She didn't reply, just returned to her knitting.

He touched his hat and moved away. He hadn't persevered with his questioning. If Johnson was staying here, another reason he might have chosen the less than salubrious establishment of Mrs Cannon was that the two of them knew each other; and he could trust her. If that was the case she'd just give JJ lies, then tell Johnson about his asking.

He moved back towards the centre of town. It might pay him to keep his eye on the livery stable. He looked back and opposite the stable he saw a saloon with a window overlooking the street. That would be a good vantage point. No point in taking up his vigil at the moment. He didn't figure Johnson would walk down the street in daylight.

He returned to the guest house, freshened up and took a meal. As the sun was setting he began the evening by sitting on a boardwalk seat some distance away but within sight of the livery. He didn't know how long this would take – after all, it was only a long shot – and he might arouse suspicions if he sat at a saloon window looking out all night.

Two boring hours later he moved down to the saloon, bought a drink and sat close to the window.

It was equally boring inside as the banjo clock on the wall ticked the evening away. At closing time he left and headed for his hotel, musing that long shots are called that because sometimes they don't pay off.

He was nearing his destination and just passing an alleyway when a voice rasped out of the darkness, 'Washington. Don't go for your irons. There's a gun already trained on your gut.'

TWELVE

'So, take it mighty easy and come into the alley a pace.'

JJ stepped into the darkness.

'A mite further than that, Mr Washington. So folks can't see us.'

'That Johnson?'

'Sure is.'

'What's this all about?'

'I know you had a rep with a gun – once – but don't do nothing that'll make me jerk this trigger finger. You can't see much of me in the dark, whereas you're outlined plain against the light.'

'I know that. What do you want with me?'

'Funny. I want to know the same thing. Why you asking after me?'

'Old Ma Cannon, I suppose.'

'Never mind how I know. Quit stalling and

answer my question. I know the pesky sheriff's got me in his sights but why you dogging me? You ain't the law – you gave up your badge years ago – and I've ain't done you no harm as I recall.'

'True. And I'm not the law. I was hired on a private basis.'

'By who?'

'Archie Royal.'

Johnson laughed in disbelief. 'Archie Royal? That old washerwoman of a man. What's he got to do with this can of worms?'

'He got a message you were after revenge; that you'd got a grudge against him for identifying you at your trial.'

Johnson laughed again. 'Hell, I'll admit I wouldn't cry at his funeral but I ain't got no gripe against him in particular. Shucks, if I was after vengeance on that score I'd have to wipe out half the town. Hell, give me credit for some sense, Mr Washington. Ain't no profit in that.'

'That's what I thought.'

'OK, so why you still after me? They

posted a bounty on me already?'

'Not as far as I know. Fact is, like I said, I got a deal with Royal. To earn my money I need to take you in so that the air can be cleared, one way or another.'

'Well, I'm telling you now. He's safe from me.'

'Then there's Deputy Talbot.'

'I didn't kill the lawman.'

'I wouldn't expect you to say anything different.'

'I'm talking the truth, mister. It was one of Crawford's boys, not me. I'd got a bone to pick with Crawford on account of something that happened when I came out the slammer. I went visiting him, but his heavies didn't cotton to me being there. I knocked out the lamp and was making my escape when the lawman turned up. I figure in the darkness they thought it was me and blasted him. Next thing I know, they'd fixed it so it looked like I was the killer. Mighty convenient two ways.'

'Why two ways?'

'Blaming me gets them off the hook for shooting down the lawman. Plus, framing me for the killing gives Crawford what looks like a legitimate reason for him or his boys to plant me, no questions asked.'

By now JJ's eyes had fully dilated in the darkness and he could make out Johnson quite clearly; and the gun he was holding. 'I don't get it. Why would he want you planted?'

'The business I had with Crawford that I was telling you about.'

'What's that?'

'For some reason he sent out some gunnies to get me just after I got out of the pen. The bastard put a contract on me.'

'That'd be the two stiffs found out on the trail near Tie Siding?'

Johnson smiled. 'That's them. Frigging amateurs.'

'Why did he want you out of the way?'

'Don't know. That's why I came to town and went a-calling on him. I wanted to know before I...'

He stopped but JJ finished his sentence. '...Before you wiped Crawford out.'

'If you want to put it that way. Hell, he had it coming for sending those two critters after me, trying to make me a man with no future.'

'And you've still got no idea why he wanted you planted?'

'No. Before I could get anything out of him all hell broke loose.'

'The robbery you got put away for – it's my figuring you and he were in cahoots on the job. This present business could be something to do with that.'

'Don't see how. That caper's a done deal, water under the bridge. Neither of us has reason for any recriminations against the other. In fact, if anything, he owes me for not grassing on him. Hell, I could have got a lighter sentence if I'd turned State's Evidence on him. But I kept my trap shut.'

'Honour amongst thieves?'

'If you say so.'

'OK, maybe he just wanted to keep you

quiet permanent. As long as you're alive you could finger him for the job.'

'Don't make sense. If I hadn't talked in three years, he'd know there ain't no reason for me to spill the beans now.'

'What about the take from the bank heist? Maybe there's some leftover business about the take?'

Johnson laughed. 'That's the hell of it. The caper was all for nothing. The stuff got burnt.'

JJ mouthed a long 'mmm', then: 'I know it looks that way but I've had enough years in the crook-catching business to know it ain't too difficult to make it look like there's no money. Won't be the first time a caper's been rigged so it look like there's no proceeds left to fight over. That way the dust can settle on a job with nobody nosing.'

'You can think what you like, mister. Makes no never mind to me. All I know, I've served my time. I rode out of the pen with a clean slate. Next thing I know I'm having to blast my way out of trouble and end up in the middle of some kind of mess I don't understand. And now I'm getting framed for killing a deputy.'

'For what it means, I think there's some truth in what you say.'

Johnson gave a snort. 'You figure I give a rat's ass what you think?' He threw glances up and down the alley. 'All I want to do now is get out of town with nobody on my back-trail. Not you, not the sheriff, not nobody.'

'It ain't as easy as that, Johnson, and you know it.'

'What's that mean?'

'I'm taking you in.'

Johnson shook his head. 'I can't believe you're talking like that,' he said with a monumental degree of scepticism in his voice. 'I'm holding all the cards here, pal, if you hadn't noticed. I got a gun pointed slam at your middle while I'm in the dark and you're silhouetted like some shooting gallery target at the county carny. OK, you was a bounty hunter once. But even in your prime you couldn't get the best of me in this situation. And certainly not now – at your age. Hell, I've seen you walk around town. You're as stiff as a board. Them fingers of yourn will be likewise.'

He paused, then: 'Listen, I don't want to kill you, old-timer. You just promise to stay off my back and you can walk out of this on your stiff legs. And I ride out of town like nothing has happened. That way we're both–'

He got no further. JJ dropped into a crouch while, as if by magic, Navy Colts were in his hands, and the alley echoed with gunfire. One shot went straight into Johnson's gun, forcing it out of his hand before he could trigger it, while the second clipped his other arm; and he slumped sideways crashing through an unlocked door. Inside he lay on the floor wincing in pain.

'I don't believe it,' he mouthed, his face against the floorboards. He meant it; he'd never seen guns drawn so fast. Everything he'd said about the old man's capabilities counted for zilch.

JJ moved quickly into the frame of the door. But in the blackness of the interior he could barely make out the form of the man.

Johnson could smell wood shavings. He'd fallen into a carpenter's store. He turned over and gripped his arm while his mind raced. 'Making a play like that against a man with a gun already drawn and cocked – you're either nuts or a master.'

He groaned loud as though preoccupied with his wound and what had happened to him. 'I heard tell they called you the Gunmaster once,' he said, playing for time. 'Hell, after that, you're still the Gunmaster, Mr Washington.'

'Cut the flattery,' JJ said, 'and get on your feet. Like I said, I'm walking you down to the law office.'

Johnson pretended it required great effort to stagger to his feet. With his face downturned, he made a show of his limp left arm while his right hand probed the surface of what felt like a workbench at his other side.

'Come on,' JJ urged. 'You ain't that badly

hit. I aimed only to scratch you.'

Johnson's fingers sensed some chunky discarded tool on the bench, felt like a woodman's plane. He gripped it and let his arm slip behind his back. There was no way the old man would see it, given the darkness of the wood-shop and the way the two men were positioned.

'OK, I'm coming.'

He lurched back into the alley. But as he turned to walk along it, he used the natural impetus of the movement to bring up his right hand, smashing the ex-bounty hunter across the temple. The old man fell forward and Johnson brought the heavy plane down on the back of his head.

He bent down and checked the man was no longer a threat. 'Gunmaster, maybe, Mr Washington,' he breathed over the body, 'but getting the best in a situation ain't all guns.' His own weapon probably unusable – he had not time to check – he took one of JJ's fallen guns and slipped it into his holster.

THIRTEEN

Jim Taggart was checking the horses were OK for the night when he thought he heard gunfire. Neighing and stomping of hoofs indicated the animals had heard it too. Not too far away from the sound of it. He dismissed the noise and was just about to lock the livery stable door when Ham Johnson loomed out of the darkness.

'Like to take my hoss, Mr Taggart,' he said. 'You help me to saddle up?'

'Sure.'

'You hear some gunfire just now?' the hostler said, as he hauled the saddle off its stand.

'Yeah. Saw it too. Couple of rowdies rough-housing as they came out of the saloon. Kids today – stupid peckerheads. Throwing lead like that they could have hurt somebody.'

'How much do I owe?' he asked, when his mount was kitted out.

'Nothing. You paid in advance, remember? In fact, I owe you some change.'

The man heaved himself up. 'That's OK, kid. Keep it.'

And with that he was gone.

Jim finished his locking up and headed down the street on his way home. Passing an alley he heard groaning. He looked into the darkness. There was a shape on the ground. Hesitantly he edged into the gloom. There was little breeze and the whiff of cordite could still be sensed on the night air.

Reaching the form he knelt down. 'Mr Washington!'

JJ groaned and opened his eyes, recognizing the speaker. 'You seen Ham Johnson?'

'Why, yes. He's just collected his horse and left town. This – it was his doing?'

'Yeah. I gotta get after him.'

'You don't look in a fit state to go nowhere, Mr Washington. I figure the best place for you is the doc's.'

'Ain't got time. You see which way he went?'

'No, but as I was locking up I heard him galloping down the street, westward out of town. Then, it being a quiet night and sound travelling easy, I figure he swung up the northern trail.'

'Right. Give me a hand to my hoss, kid.'

'You don't look capable of riding, Mr Washington.'

JJ started to haul himself to his feet. 'How I look and what I'm capable of are two different things.'

Taggart helped him to stand and move along the alley. 'I don't think...' he began.

'OK, I'll manage alone,' JJ grunted, as they neared the end of the passage.

'Well, if you insist,' the young man conceded.

'Better still,' JJ said, when they emerged into the relative light of the street, 'can you give me loan of a couple of horses, strong ones?' His slowly returning faculties were telling him he could have a long ride ahead. 'My own's not as sturdy as he was.'

In his bounty-hunting days he always travelled with two. The inexperienced owl-hoot would only use one horse, reckoning one was faster and more manoeuvrable. Which was true. But only over short distances. For the long haul, two beat one hands down. A brace of horses moved more slowly but spelling them in turn gave far greater endurance. Plus, a tow horse enabled rations to be carried.

'No problem. You're speaking to the right man. Horses is my line, Mr Washington. I can think of a couple of beauts. Good runners; and will be docile under a strange rider.'

Within minutes JJ was to find that Jim Taggart chancing upon him was doubly adventitious.

After the hostler had helped him into his house and explained events to his wife, the young lady stood back and said, 'Why, I do believe it's Mr Washington, isn't it?'

'You have the advantage of me, ma'am.'

'Before Jim and I were wed I used to live in Dry Gulch. You keep a store there.'

'That's right, ma'am.'

'In fact, my ma bought the material for my wedding dress from your very place.'

From then she fussed over him like a mother hen, with talk about her home town. While Jim caparisoned the horses, she bathed JJ's head wounds, then prepared a more than ample supply of food for whatever journey he intended.

An hour later he was mounted up with a well-stocked tow horse to his rear. Jim had leant him a replacement handgun and, from his guest house, had fetched his trusty Winchester which now nestled snugly in the saddle boot.

'You sure you're going to be OK?' Mrs Taggart asked with genuine concern.

'Yes, ma'am. And thank you for your consideration. If this caper works out, you get Jim to bring you over to the store and you'll be able to take your pick from a wide range of choice fabrics. On the house.'

After he had made his goodbyes and disappeared into the darkness, Jim hurried over to the smithy and woke up Big John to acquaint him with the news.

Pulling on his pants and shirt the blacksmith went with Jim to the law office to put the sheriff in the picture.

The lawman looked at the clock. 'It's after midnight,' he yawned. 'Ain't no way I can pull a posse together at this hour. Can't get anything organized till morning.'

'But that'll be another seven, eight hours,' Big John protested. 'Anything could have happened by then.'

'Best I can offer.'

The lawman closed the door and hauled himself back up the stairs. 'Eight hours?' he muttered to his sleeping wife, as he doused the lantern and snuggled under the bedsheets. 'Knowing this town – more like ten hours. Or longer. By then can't see it worth setting out at all.'

FOURTEEN

JJ rode for several hours but from time to time dizziness returned and eventually he had to pull in to bivouac. He couldn't track in the dark anyway, he told himself. Besides, maybe some hours sleep would improve his condition. And the forward-thinking Mrs Taggart had supplied him with blankets.

Come daybreak he was awake. His head still felt like it had been stuck in a vice but there was noticeable improvement. Again, thanks to the beneficences of the lady Taggart he had food and refreshing coffee.

He mounted up. The one thing he hoped was that Johnson had had to rest up too. But from the outset the hunter had been travelling blind, just heading north; and the further he journeyed the greater the chance that his prey had angled off in a new direction.

He had taken up the pursuit impetuously, with his mind clouded in anger. Now in the cold light of day the rational part of his brain turned his thinking to the possibility that at some time he would have to give up.

By mid-morning he noted tiredness in his mount. 'You and me, brother,' he said as he dropped out of the saddle at the edge of a river. He gave the horses a break from their burden and let them drink. But after he had exchanged the loads between saddle and pack horse, his knees melted. He mouthed an expletive as he dropped his backside onto a rock and took off his hat. He wetted his forehead and neck in an attempt to revive himself. He rested for a while, watching the occasional freshly-cut log swinging down-stream. Eventually he mounted up and headed out once more, following the course of the river.

His head was throbbing and his spirits were low. His demeanour remained in a slough until there came a couple of turns in his fortune.

His first break, a small one, came when he spotted, on the other side of the river, the lumber camp responsible for the logs he had seen. With the sound of sawing and chopping there was hell of a racket going on but during a pause in the cacophony he shouted across the torrent. Had anyone seen a lone rider heading north? One of them shouted they'd seen one at a distance. There was enough in his description to suggest that it might be Johnson.

He changed direction a little to work his way across to where the sighted rider was likely to have travelled. But another notion was clouding his thoughts – had the years robbed him of his tracking skill? Some; but there were still vestiges; enough for him to follow a trail if he could only have a good break. The joints might be seizing up but there were some things that hadn't changed. Memories of his manhunting days surfaced as he dropped out of the saddle to study the ground. Flattened grass here, a hoof-scraped rock there.

Then came the good break. He not only found a hoof print but he knew it was the mark of the horse that carried his quarry. Out of simple instinct when he had come across the unfamiliar horse in the livery – the one that had proved to be Johnson's – he had examined the hoofs. It had been a purely automatic action, but now it paid off. The combination of nicks and wear in the four hoofs attested that the animal that had come this way was without doubt the grey.

Rejuvenated, he pressed on.

Now he had found something definite he picked up pace.

'The guy's getting lazy,' he said to himself some time later, when he noted Johnson was now keeping to an established trail. 'Must think he's done enough switchbacking to confuse anybody who might be following.'

The terrain became rougher as he approached the Medicine Bow Mountains, the trail threading through notches in hills. Whenever he approached a rim he would dismount a few paces before and venture a look over. You didn't offer your quarry the convenience of your being limned against the skyline.

Suddenly, his ageing but still eagle eyes spotted a speck of whiteness in the grass. He dropped down. A cigarette butt. He examined it and smiled. It hadn't been discarded long. Had to have been some time this very day. Dropped the previous day, although now dry, it would have become soaked in dew overnight, the tobacco staining it brown. The paper on this little baby was still white.

Feeling less pressure now, he nooned under a stand of trees near a stream. He finished with coffee and a cigar, and resumed his tracking with renewed confidence and energy.

As he progressed, the landscape was becoming littered with boulders, some the size of houses. Eventually, he came to point where the trail brimmed over a low summit and led into a cleft in the terrain. He approached cautiously, noticing how the valley rose on all sides to jagged summits.

More important in the distance he could make out a dismounted figure. On foot he worked his way sidewards until he could lead his horses over the brow of the rise using the cover of trees. From thence he descended down a juniper-blanketed slope and advanced along the side of the valley, taking advantage of whatever rock or vegetation afforded protection.

JJ tethered the horses out of sight. Pulling out the Winchester he edged closer. By the time he had got in proximity to the man's horse, the rider himself had disappeared. Where?

Inching closer still, he heard scraping sounds above, the noise of rocks being slung. What was going on?

The chunky sounds indicated that the man was somewhere up in the rocks. JJ made a quick reconnaissance of the area then worked his way upwards so that he could circle round and then be able to look down on the likely location. When he had done so, he saw the man. It was Johnson. And he was scrabbling about in a crevice, now and then hurling small rocks, this way and that, oblivious to where they landed.

Eventually the toiler gave up the task and went to the edge of a granite rampart. He flung a final rock into the void, shouting an expletive that echoed around the valley.

JJ lined up his gun. 'Hey, Johnson,' he yelled. 'You lose something?'

Johnson whirled round and saw the levelled gun. Having already witnessed the skill behind it he refrained from going for his own weapon.

'If you been watching me for a spell, old-timer, you'll know so.'

'The hidden loot,' JJ exclaimed.

'Yeah,' Johnson snarled.

'I know you got a rep for being hell-bent and crazy, Johnson, but don't try anything. Take out your gun with your left hand and sling it.'

When the action was competed to his satisfaction, JJ instructed him to move down to the flat. As he began to follow the descending figure he picked up the discarded gun and rammed it into his belt.

'So what's going on?' JJ wanted to know when they had reached the bottom.

'It all figures now,' Johnson said, as though in a dream. 'The whole shebang.'

JJ nodded up towards the crevice. 'The money?'

The other parked his backside on a rock and looked blankly at the ground. 'Yeah. You were right when you suggested the money wasn't burnt. It was part of the plan. We fixed it that way. Set up the cabin beforehand so that it would go up. Threw some burnt bills around, then divvied up and went our separate ways. I headed up here and buried my cut. Red must have followed me and seen where I stashed it; then, when I got took by the tin stars and was out of the way, the bastard simply helped himself to it.'

'A stroke of luck for him, you being the only one caught.'

'Yeah,' Johnson mused, as it sank in. 'The

way things are turning out, seems the bastard could have had a hand in that too. Anyways, me being penned-up meant he was safe, at least for a spell. Yeah, it all fits. My take along with his would have given him the dough to set up that Lodge outfit back in town. Huh, the short-ass bozo always wanted to be a big honcho. Now he's one of the biggest in the county.'

'You know, I don't figure that place. I know these secret societies – Freemasons, Teutonic Knights and such – are disliked by ordinary folk and a mite suspect with their patting of each other's backs, but I never heard of them being downright crook.'

Johnson chuckled. 'Red Crawford has never been straight in his life. You can bet your bottom dollar that that place is a cover for something. Now he's the big cheese he's always wanted to be, I'm just a fly in the ointment. Only trouble is, I ain't as easy to swat as a blue-assed fly.'

There was a dawning comprehension in JJ's eyes. 'And your stash being missing explains why he wanted you dead as soon as you got out.'

'Yeah, he wanted me out of the picture before I found out it had gone. That's why he tried to fix a hit on me as soon as I got released. He knew once I'd found out that it had disappeared I'd be gunning for him and his wormy life wouldn't be worth a wooden nickel. Maybe me coming out early explains why it was such a rush job. If him and Arnold had had more time, I figure they should have been able to get more capable shootists to do the job.'

He stood up, sighed deep as the facts sunk in, and looked up and down the valley. Then, in a changed tone of voice: 'What you gonna do now?'

'Like I been telling you. Take you in.'

Johnson grunted in a startled fashion. 'What for? I told you I didn't kill the deputy. Hell, don't you believe me?'

'Maybe. But if you didn't, you're the only one who can help nail Crawford and his gunnies for it. The thing needs rectifying and Crawford needs to be brought to account. Maybe it's because I was a lawman once and can't get it out of my blood. Besides, you're pegged as the deputy's killer. You'll be on the run for the rest of your life. There'll be no state or territory you can hide in. It'll be best for you to come back with me and get your slate cleared.'

'No. There's a red-headed bastard got a debt to pay before I do anything else.'

'When the story's out, he'll get his dues.'

'Ain't good enough for me.'

JJ waggled his gun. 'No, you're coming in with me.' He smiled. 'And don't worry about the other matters.'

'What other matters?'

'The two stiffs out on the trail. And Josh Arnold. There's no witnesses or evidence, so no case. And from the way this story is panning out, they asked for it. You're a hard man and, the way I see it, anybody tries to do the dirty on you for their own ends, they take their chances.'

Suddenly the feeling of wooziness returned,

and now it was his turn to sit on a rock. But as he did so he ensured that he kept his gun levelled. 'Besides, there's a personal reason for getting you back. I told you before. I'm being paid to protect Archie Royal from you. I go back empty handed, the case is still open and I mightn't get my money.'

Johnson laughed. 'And I told you. I was never after him. Crawford rigged all that. He knew Archie Royal is a nervous old cuss. Everybody does. He knew he'd go running to the law if it could be put about I was after him. That way, before anything happens it gets laid down that I'm looking for trouble. Then, anybody gets shot up, I'm going to be the chief suspect on the sheriff's list.'

At that point he began to study his captor. He could see the man was wavering. Not just his head but his eyes. Looked like he was having trouble focusing. Then Johnson remembered the heavy blows he had laid on the man's head in making his escape. He smiled to himself. No need to plead his case any longer. He would play along with the fellow for a spell. The state the oldster was in, he'd be easy to jump.

There was lots of time. Maybe in an hour or so...

But he didn't have to wait that long. Suddenly the bounty hunter keeled over and slumped heavily to the ground.

FIFTEEN

When JJ came to he was lying on the ground and all the weaponry was in the possession of the ex-convict.

JJ shook his head and eased himself up a little to lean on an elbow. 'How come you're still here?' he asked, when he realized where he was and what had happened.

'The situation is you're not taking me in. I'm lighting out of the territory. But seems to me you're in urgent need of a doc. Shucks, it'll be no skin of my ass to tote you along until we find one. It's the least I can do for an old coot as dogged as you are. I respect that.' He reflected a moment. 'That is on one condition.'

'And that is...?'

'It's my figuring you're saddled with the inconvenience of being an honourable man. So, you give me your word that when I leave you in some medic's capable hands you don't sashay round to the nearest law office and get them on my tail.'

JJ had no choice. It was either do as Johnson suggested – and the man was right: if he gave his word he would keep it – or try to get someplace by himself and probably fall out of the saddle.

'I have a condition too.'

Johnson laughed. 'Your brain really has been affected, old timer. You ain't in no position to make conditions!'

'I know, so let's call it a request.'

Johnson chuckled and went along with the game. 'OK, go on.'

'Whatever you do, you keep clear of

Julesburg, so Archie Royal don't get scared again. Otherwise, I'll never get back to my missus and store.'

'OK, you old buzzard. I don't mind bending a mite. But the best thing you're gonna get from me is a half-promise.'

'Half? I don't get you.'

'I don't go back in the near future. That should keep your Mr Royal happy till the dust settles. But I'll be back sometime. I got a score to settle with Crawford. And he knows it. He's always gonna be looking over his shoulder, wondering when he's gonna get the bullet. That way it appeals to me not to rush back. While I'm away I'll enjoy the notion of him sweating. But when the time comes, ain't nothing gonna stop me from settling his hash. Now come on. No more fancy talk. The sooner we're eating trail the better for both of us.'

He helped JJ into the saddle and they headed north.

After some miles there was still no signs of

habitation. JJ had told him about the supplies he was toting so they pulled in for a rest and bite to eat.

'I been thinking,' JJ said, as they sipped coffee round a fire. 'If by some quirk of fate the situation gets reversed, I've dropped the notion of taking you in.'

'Gee, that sure is a weight off my mind,' the other said, with an ironic chuckle.

'I'm just putting my cards on the table. You could have left me. I have to be thankful for that. Everybody's got you pegged as a hell-bent crazy man but there's more to you than that. You've served your time for the bank robbery. And all the mayhem you seem to have wrought since you came out was thrust on you. And I'm pretty sure you didn't kill the deputy. OK, you've done some bad things but only to no-goods who themselves are prepared to do anything to get their way.'

Johnson stood up, slung the dregs from his coffee mug. 'Quit your sermonizing, Mr Washington, or I'll have second thoughts about getting your ass to a doc. One thing you have to know about me before we go any further: I just hate preachifying.'

He doused the fire from a nearby stream. 'Come on, pa. Let's git.'

He'd just repacked the gear and was about to help JJ into the saddle when a shot rang out. He staggered down the grade and splashed into the stream.

Trying to locate the source of the shot, JJ limped as fast as he could down the slope after him. He turned the man over. A round from a high-powered rifle had taken a chunk out of the back of Johnson's head. He pulled his Navy Colt from the dead man's holster and scanned the environs. The shot had come from the south of them.

And so did the next fusillade.

With bullets whizzing around him he bounded as best he could up the grade, claiming weaponry as he crossed the site. Finally pulling the Winchester from its boot, he headed for the cover of the nearest rocks.

He just made them when another bullet

zinged into the hard surface beside him, sending a shower of rock shards into his face.

Either there had been a natural improvement or adrenalin was doing its work but his dizziness was now minimal, allowing his brain to pick up speed. This had to be Red Crawford and his mob. He was the only one who would know where Johnson had been headed. And he wouldn't stop at squashing Johnson. He'd have to eliminate the old bounty-hunter; the gang boss would know it was highly likely that Johnson would have put him in the picture about the missing money – and who was involved in the bank heist, its original source.

Thankfully there was good cover and he worked his way up between the rocks. Keeping out of sight so the bushwhackers could not locate him, he reached a high vantage point, took off his hat and peered cautiously over a rock. Occasionally a rifle cracked roughly in his direction. He could make out three. He worked his way upwards and further back so that he was getting close to them.

When facing such odds experience taught him not to fire injudiciously. Otherwise he would be pinpointed to no advantage. By watching the source of the shots and catching the occasional glimpse of a moving figure he now put the tally at four.

Considerable opposition for a lesser man but not an overwhelming number in his healthy, younger days. But now...?

He checked the Winchester was fully loaded but deliberately stayed his hand, listening, content to wait for his opportunity, through the muted drone of insects, the occasional breaking of twigs, the scratch of rocks underfoot. Then he saw what he was looking for: two of the critters. His one advantage at the moment was they didn't quite know where he was – so he could take his time. He lined up on the most difficult of the two targets; that was the one that required some application. His gun carefully tracked the moving figure, while simultaneously he kept himself aware of the position of the second one. That way, when he fired the first considered shot, he could swing swiftly and with some precision to the easier mark.

He paused a few seconds longer, then *bam*. A well-controlled swing to the second, and *bam*.

He ducked down, chunks of rock splintering around him as somebody located his muzzle flare. The elevation was getting steeper and as he scrabbled for some decent cover, a chunk of rock broke under his boot. It caused him to slip down a couple of yards. He wasn't injured but falling debris created a racket that brought more lead in his direction. He thought on his situation. Reckoning they would anticipate his upward movement to continue, he backtracked.

He chanced a glance and, with satisfaction, could see he had downed his two targets. Only two to go.

But – hell – the dizziness was creeping over him again.

His concentration ebbing fast, he rested. Jeez, he wasn't going to black out again? Minutes passed. He could near nothing. Weakly he wormed his way down to another vantage point. Hazarding a look over the rocks he suddenly saw a figure directly opposite on the other side of the valley. The red hair told him it was Crawford. JJ could tell by the shift of the head that the man was scanning the terrain, confused by the echoing and re-echoing of the shots. He should be able to drop him. The gang boss was not out of range. JJ lined up, but had to shake his head to try to restore some focusing ability.

Hell, the dizziness was reasserting itself with a vengeance.

Then he heard a crunch of rock behind and above him. There was the sound of loose scree falling. He jerked his aching head round to see a shape high in the rocks, lining up. He recognized the figure of Beaudine, the young hardcase with the tattoo. The lad was grinning, deliberately prolonging the moment, savouring the preliminaries to the act of delivering the *coup de grâce* to yet another defenceless living thing.

Completely without protection and his own gun pointing in the wrong direction, the ex-bounty hunter didn't stand a chance.

For a moment time seemed to stand still. An eternity that was shattered by a gunshot. But the sound didn't emanate from the muzzle of the Rebel's gun. Instead the devil dancing in the desperado's eyes disappeared, to be replaced by a look of bewilderment. He let the rifle fall from his hands and he pitched forward. In its descent the body turned to crash spine-downward with a loud crack against a sharp edge of rock in a formation close to JJ.

What the...?

JJ threw a quick glance around. Then, further along the shelf on which seconds before had stood the tattooed youngster another outline appeared. A shape that JJ also recognized: Big John.

Then the bullets spanging into the rocky

face below the blacksmith wrenched JJ's attention back to his most recent target. Across the void, Crawford was trying to make a retreat, firing as he did so.

Two fast-fired rounds from the hunter's Winchester were enough to send the erst-while gang leader caroming backwards; then slithering with the loose scree to land in an undignified heap at the bottom.

'How come you turned up?' JJ asked, when the blacksmith had finally made the descent to join him.

Big John explained how Jim Taggart had informed him of the night's events and how the sheriff deemed it unworkable to get a posse together until the morning. 'By which time I figured it might be too late,' he concluded. 'So here I am.'

'I didn't know you toted a gun.'

'I don't. When I heard the racket of gun-fire and could see what the situation was, I snuck up on one at the rear and...' He balled a hand into a sledgehammer fist and brought it down. 'Don't know what damage I did. He didn't know what hit him. Anyways he had no use for his weapons anymore, so I helped myself. Managed to drop another jasper with one of his guns.'

'I knew of four making the attack but...'

'Four? With the two I downed that makes six.' He grinned. 'Six to one – I reckoned maybe odds too big even for you!'

After JJ had brought the blacksmith up to date on what had happened they went round checking the bodies. They were all dead except the one that Big John had fisted. And he was still dazed from the smith's blow when they roped him up.

'What's your name?' JJ asked, when the guy's brain was back in some resemblance of working order.

'Seth. Seth Coolridge.'

'OK, Seth. You're the only one left. And you're going to take your share of punishment for everything the Crawford gang's done. Couple of murders for a start. Now a good lawyer might save your neck from the noose, but even if he does you're going to be put away for quite a spell. So, you've only got yourself one option. First, there was Deputy Talbot. One of the gang shot Talbot in the Lodge. That's what I've been told. Now that's not direct evidence but it's a start. So, was that you?'

'No. It was Leroy.'

'OK. Just now, one of you gunned down Ham Johnson. That's murder number two.'

'That wasn't me either. It was Beaudine. I seed him.'

'There's other matters gotta be cleared up. For instance, Crawford was using the Lodge for a cover, wasn't he?'

'That's right. He organized jobs out of state. After a caper the gang would hightail it back to Julesburg to hide out in the Lodge. Red designed the place from scratch. It had lots of hidey-holes built into it in case the law came nosing. I can show you.'

'The last operation was the Denver railroad job, wasn't it?'

'Yeah.'

'Now you're gonna testify in court to all that you've just said. That way you should get some commutation of sentence. And just in case you have second thoughts, you're not going to be able to wriggle out of it.' He threw a glance at Big John. 'My friend here is a witness to your statement.'

Coolidge shook his head in resignation. 'Anything you say. I've had enough.'

They made some preparation to leave, then JJ took Big John on one side. 'Before we head back, we bury Johnson,' he said. 'I made a promise to him about not taking him in. I know there's probably some reward on his hide by now, but a promise is a promise. The man being dead don't alter that.'

'What can we say about not bringing the body back?'

'We'll think up something.'

Big John nodded. 'The river's high with spring run off. When he got shot he fell in, didn't he? Got washed plumb away.'

JJ nodded. 'That'll do. Anyways, we're not going back empty-handed. For the killings and heists that's gonna be tied to Crawford and his Lodge outfit, there's likely to be rewards or bounties on offer. We'll divvy up whatever we pull.'

'I didn't hightail it out here for the sake of money, JJ.'

'I know you didn't. Just look on it as payment for a good day's work. And that reminds me. The day's work isn't finished. You're gonna have to fix all these bozos to their horses. I don't cotton to not pulling my weight, but I don't think I got the strength for the chore.'

'No problem. You OK for riding?'

'If we take it easy.'

Some time later they were riding side by side, well on their way home, their grisly cargoes snaking out behind them. They were taking it easy, JJ was savouring a cigar, their saddle horses being allowed to set their own pace.

'What are your plans, JJ?' Big John asked. 'Maybe getting back in the saddle to chase the big bucks again?'

JJ rolled his eyes and vaguely indicated his still sore head. 'You must be joshing. Ain't no way I'm going through anything like this again.'

'A minor setback. You'll get over a head bump. Think about it. You've proved there's life in the old dog yet.'

JJ eyed him in mock reproof. 'Thanks for labelling me an "an old dog", my friend.' Then he smiled. 'No, this little operation has certainly not reopened a door. I'm too old for this stuff now. Those days are well and truly behind me. Besides, I've made a promise to my old gal. This caper was strictly a one-off and I keep my word.'

He took a final draw on what was left of his cigar and flicked it aside. 'Mind, extra funds always come in handy. Me and the missus could do with some more money to invest in our place.' He thought awhile. 'And that gives me an idea.'

'Gonna tell me about it?'

'As it involves you, I think I'd better.

Listen, you can take that so-called Killer Garfield. I've made a sum on this caper, so I got some dollars to spare. My suggestion is this. We set up a re-match with the critter. But this time I'll be your manager, set up the deal and we go fifty/fifty. Serving in the store don't take all my time. I'll book the venue so we get a cut from the thing from the off. Trouble is, you were too drugged up to remember much or to make any assessment of his capabilities. But, believe me, in a fair fight he's not in your league. Now, I've been in enough scraps in my time; not in the ring, but I was no stranger to fisticuffs in my younger days. Came with the job.

'Although the last bout didn't last long, I saw enough of Garfield to spot his flaws. I'll train you to take advantage of them. So the prize-money will be as good as ours. Plus, as you lost your first fight the odds will be against you. That fact will be in our favour. Knowing you will win, we can clean up on a big bet. What do you figure?'

The pugilist struck a boxing pose and

slammed a balled fist into the air. 'I figure yes. The other night was the first time I ever been whipped in the ring – and I didn't like it.'

'Come on then, big boy. We've got some training to do.'

'Lead me to the punch-bag, boss, and never mind the Marquis of Queensberry.' He raised both mallet fists high. *'Marquis?* This time I'll show Garfield a pair of real *dukes!'*

The publishers hope that this book has given you enjoyable reading. Large Print Books are especially designed to be as easy to see and hold as possible. If you wish a complete list of our books please ask at your local library or write directly to:

Dales Large Print Books
Magna House, Long Preston,
Skipton, North Yorkshire.
BD23 4ND

This Large Print Book, for people who cannot read normal print, is published under the auspices of
THE ULVERSCROFT FOUNDATION

... we hope you have enjoyed this book. Please think for a moment about those who have worse eyesight than you ... and are unable to even read or enjoy Large Print without great difficulty.

You can help them by sending a donation, large or small, to:

The Ulverscroft Foundation,
1, The Green, Bradgate Road,
Anstey, Leicestershire, LE7 7FU,
England.
or request a copy of our brochure for more details.

The Foundation will use all donations to assist those people who are visually impaired and need special attention with medical research, diagnosis and treatment.

Thank you very much for your help.